C000320026

ADVENTURES OF A LONDON CALL BOY

BEN FRANCKX

Published by Accent Press Ltd – 2009
ISBN 9781906373665

Printed and bound in the UK

Cover design by
The Design House

Chapter One

It was a complete accident that I became a gigolo. In fact, I don't even like the word. 'Gigolo' sounds kitsch, like we're stuck in the Seventies, and makes me sound like I should have a greasy 'tache (I don't). 'Male prostitute' sounds a bit too much like I'm up before a judge, and 'rent-boy', well, the rainbow village got there first, and I wouldn't want to give anyone the wrong idea.

'Call boy', or 'call guy', is much better, and if I'm ever asked to provide a job title that's probably what I'll pick. But most of the time, it simply needs a woman to call up and ask me, 'You fuck for money, right?'

Sometimes I'll reply, sometimes just a nod you can't see. The result, of course, is always the same.

'Uh huh. If that's how you want to put it.'

So I'll be honest with you: I'm not particularly boastful about my recent career change but I'm not ashamed about it either. But let's just say that if you introduce me to your friends, please don't start by saying, 'Hey, this is Cesc, he sleeps with women on a fixed-fee basis.' Unless you say it quietly and with the possibility of some work as a result.

It was my friend Celeste who came up with the fixed-fee thing. I'd wanted to have a scale, based on whether I found the lady in question attractive or not. Sorry, that should be 'client', because this is a service industry, after all. But Celeste insisted that would be discriminatory and, what was worse, customers might talk to each other. It would be terrible to discover that your paid shag charged extra because the job was less enjoyable and even worse for me if one of them ever confronted me

1

over variable charges.

What I *do* have rates for is different services. It's fairly simple now but at the beginning I had no idea. You know there's no City & Guilds for male sex workers.

Just sex, I would say, is generally affordable. Obviously travel and any expenses are extra, and it's by the hour, give or take five minutes or so. Orgasms aren't priced, which is not to say that they're priceless. I've just never got round to quantifying: would a multiple bucking bronco oral-cum cost more than a knee-trembler from behind, for example? Generally I always come, at least once, and indeed quite a few clients seem to enjoy the visibility of the male orgasm. I never realised that some women get their sex education from porn too.

There are no surcharges for characters, fantasies or disguises: it's considered part of the service. If you want to be possessed by an Italian count or ravished by Mr Darcy, I can oblige, although the accents, well, you can take or leave them. I do Spanish well, for reasons I'll explain as we go along.

Dates take longer and are therefore more expensive, but sex is guaranteed. I give a discount for a full night but generally women don't really want to wake up with hired staff like me. One bonus is a guaranteed good night's sleep, if you want it, or guaranteed no sleep if you don't.

I have also in the past given discounts for group bookings. I would do so again.

So in many respects, it's a very pleasant job. Like I said, it's a fixed fee, and generally work, or Janes or Jennies as some of them rather jokingly call themselves, gets to me by word of mouth. I don't just do sex (in all its varieties), either; I'm presentable, charming, so I'm

2

told, dress well, and can be relied upon to fake knowledge of a number of different professions, so can also be hired for weddings, work dos and, on one occasion, a funeral. I look good in black, OK.

Why do I do it? The sex is obviously an advantage. A very cynical friend of mine, a guy called Archie, occasional frequenter of lady prostitutes, argued that he might as well pay up front as in the end it worked out cheaper. You pay for it one way or another, he argued, whether she's a whore or not. But I take a professional approach: your pleasure is my aim, and if you enjoy it, then I enjoy it. If mutual predilections happen to coincide, that's simply happy chance.

The good thing about being a professional is that women always make an effort. I guess it's because they're paying. Grey knickers, stray pubes, chewed nails all go out of the window: when they're buying you get agent provocateur, smooth waxed stripes and Brazilians, French manicures, the works. Some women, it seems, go to very great trouble. One client had herself shaved into a 'C', just for me. I was impressed.

The other advantage is the independence: I don't have a boss, although I think that Celeste has secretly been trying to manage my business on the sly. My efforts are paid in cash (shh, don't tell anyone, OK). I can work pretty much when I want, although, as you'd guess, most of the real business goes on at night. But you'd be surprised. I've graced a handful of offices with my services during the day, disguised as a client for a secret hush-hush meeting, ahem, over the office table. I guess it shows the way the world is changing: women aren't ashamed to spend money on what they want, and guaranteed good sex is high on the list. Luckily, that's where I come in.

I should probably also mention that the work is pretty much seasonal. In my two years or so at it – excuse the expression – I've noticed the way the job tends to ebb and flow. The summer months generally aren't so busy. I guess that women look their best with all the tanning, gymming and waxing they do for the summer. The sun and the sundresses get guys' peckers up, and the girls go away for racy weeks of sand and sex. So there's less need for my trade. But once the clocks have gone back and entertainment is reduced to drinking with the girls or white wine in front of the TV, it seems that I come into demand to provide some fun for those lonely nights. I guess I'm a bit like buying a new vibrator for the evening, only with batteries included and wrapped precisely how you want. All of which is a way of saying that if you call me in February, you may have to wait a few days.

I suppose I should tell you a bit more about me but I'm afraid that will have to wait for the moment.

Chapter Two

After some assignments, I have to ask myself whether this is worth the trouble or not. I mean of course it is, but it's not always as easy as you might think. I'll give you an example.

I'd had a call from a landline – curious in itself, I thought, as mobiles are the way things work in this game – while I was enjoying a coffee with Celeste on the Parkway. She's an artist and part-time model, which basically means she is quirkily sexy, has too much time on her hands and has a mysterious private income.

'Sorry Cel, this looks like work,' I said, excusing myself and sitting back in my wooden chair.

'I hear you fuck for money,' said the educated female voice on the other end of the line.

'Hmmhmm,' I replied as positively as possible.

'What do you charge?'

I told her some standard rates. She found the price acceptable and gave me her details. An hour later I stepped out of a taxi on a leafy street in Mill Hill. The house was a whitewashed detached building with a gravel drive and neatly trimmed hedges. Anywhere else in the world it would be an unremarkable dwelling but in these parts it suggested the presence of millionaires. That and the two Mercs on the drive, of course. I guess I should have suspected something: who parks two Mercs on the drive during the day, after all? The suburbs are full of sexual adventurers, so they tell me.

I rang the doorbell and a gym-wife in her late forties answered. These are a special type of client, basically bored housewives who have given up fucking their

5

Pilates instructors. Most of my Jennies are professional types, but there are a few ladies of leisure who frequent my services. This woman was one of them.

'Come in,' she said. 'You're younger than I thought.'

'I just look after myself. I must say that you look very well yourself.' She did too: slim, woollen skirt over good legs, frilly blouse and elegantly bobbed light hair. Little pearl earrings, too, to which I later imagined myself adding a necklace, if I knew her type.

'Well I hope you know what you're doing,' she added, looking me up and down.

'So they tell me,' I replied with a smile.

'Would you like a drink?' she asked.

'If you insist.'

We walked through into a wide, thickly carpeted living room. She poured bourbon from a sideboard for both of us, necked hers, waited while I did likewise, and then walked towards me.

'Shall we?' she enquired.

'My pleasure.'

'No, no. *My* pleasure,' she purred, handing me an envelope.

Now people come to professionals for all sorts of reasons: some for a bit of fun, some to cure frustration, some to experiment. My suspicion in this case was that my client wanted one thing: sex tricks.

We went upstairs to a cream and silk bedroom with a large mirror in front of an emperor-sized bed. I kissed her and slowly unbuttoned her top, sitting her down on the bed. She was hard bodied and lithe, and I massaged her shoulders and back as I slipped off an expensive bra. Her breasts were tanned and freckled: quality aesthetic surgery had clearly taken place.

'By the way,' she said, as I flicked her nipple gently

with my tongue, 'do you mind if my husband watches?'

'No,' I said, without hesitation. 'Where is he? He can join in if you like.'

'No,' she said, apparently noticing me cast a sly look around the room. 'You won't even see him.'

'OK. You're the boss.'

'Too right.'

From then on I was under orders, and she got the lot: a thorough working over of her nipples and breasts, a massage of her legs and thighs and once I'd slipped off a pair of almost invisible knickers she produced a vibrator from somewhere under the bed which I put to use on her whole body.

Then I tongued the alphabet and hummed a whole set of tunes between her legs: the result was a noisy ovation. She was soon gobbling enthusiastically at my cock, before I slipped on a condom. Then she pushed me over and manoeuvred herself on top of me, admiring herself in the mirror as she flicked herself to a third or possible fourth coming while I tweaked hard on her tight nipples. She twisted around a couple of times, encouraging me to play with her buttocks from behind. Then she rolled off and shifted onto all fours, barking an order to me over her shoulder. I duly obliged with gusto.

Up until then, all fine. Until I heard a car pull up on the drive. I paused momentarily and looked in the direction of the window.

'Keep going! I'm almost there!' she shouted at me over her shoulder and through gritted teeth.

'Erm, OK,' I said, putting my back into it as she returned to groaning appreciatively. 'But you do know that someone's just parked up outside?'

'Ahh. Fuck. Whatever.'

I could tell that she wasn't paying too much attention,

and continued stroking my cock in and out of her. We were back in our stride once more, her breathing getting deeper and louder.

Until we were interrupted by the sound of the front door opening.

The client shot away from me quicker than if I'd told her I had crabs.

'Shit! It's my husband: get in there!' she hissed, pulling open what I'd thought was just a mirror.

I looked at her in confusion.

'My *real* husband,' she added.

I dived into the room as requested, and she shoved a handful of clothes towards me. I thought I'd be in a bathroom, or a cupboard. Instead, I was in a small room, comfortably decked out with plush seats and a couple of TV monitors. And what I now realised was a one-way window.

It was a viewing gallery. I was impressed. She really was an adventuress. But the sight of a slightly chubby, balding man in his fifties, semi-erect cock in hand, immediately disgusted away my erection. The door was closed and locked behind me.

'I thought you were her husband,' I whispered to him in the dark.

He laughed nervously.

'I'm her friend. It's a game. I like to watch. She lets me.'

'Clearly,' I replied. 'Look, would you mind not masturbating anymore? I find it rather off-putting.'

'Sorry. I was quite close, that's all.'

'Right. Well stop it. Particularly now I'm in here too.'

I heard voices outside. Raised voices.

'Fuck this,' I said. With a shove the door opened. I pulled on my trousers and looked for my shirt. As I did

8

so, the client entered again.

'Shit! What are you doing out? Get dressed, he's coming.' She shoved me in a random direction, coincidentally towards the window, while locking the viewing gallery with the poor voyeur inside.

'What's left of your knickers is on the floor,' I advised.

She looked like someone who'd just been interrupted during professional sex. Footsteps on the stairs brought a wave of panic.

'Quick,' she said, gesturing me towards the window. Pulling on my shirt, I found myself climbing out of the window. Luckily I'm light and strong enough, but after five minutes doing a poor impression of a Banksy, my arms gave up. I scrabbled down onto the porch roof and then down onto the patio. A third Merc was on the drive. As I scampered away and into a passing taxi, I imagined an ugly little man about to have some very difficult explaining to do; I only hoped he hadn't come. Rather him than me, although I was pissed off enough about the whole scene. It was frankly unprofessional. She could have at least told me that it was pantomime season.

Next time I'll have to tell you a bit more about me, like I promised.

Chapter Three

I said that I was going to tell you a bit about me, but I got distracted. Sorry. I'll try not to again, but it's a busy job at times.

So, here we go. I was lucky to be blessed with a number of advantages, mainly, I must admit, physical. I was born in Argentina to parents from Spain: that's why I have a name that no one can pronounce – Cesc Aleixandre, Cesc to anyone except my parents – and no one can tell where it's from. My father was in the diplomatic service, and we ended up being posted to London before I knew what was what. I guess I must have been two or three years old, max. To say that my father was an anglophile would be an understatement. Part of the deal with the diplomatic service was that I often found myself at school in a different town or even country from my parents, so I got used to a great degree of freedom as a boy, as well as never really being particularly close to my family.

What with my background, I always look slightly foreign, and don't really know what to say when people ask me where I'm from. I am, I guess, a citizen of the world, and being just a little bit exotic seems to help in this line of work. From my dad I got a tall but slim frame, dark hair, greenish-brown eyes, and a little too much body hair – don't worry, we'll deal with that later. From my mum I got dress sense and good teeth.

From neither did I get the, well, let's say equipment that you might think a man needs for this job. But let's be clear: I'm not a stripper. It's not for show. It's for a pro. Experience has taught me that charm and looks are more important than a big cock *before* we get down to business. And once we do get to the business end of things, having an average-sized member can be quite an advantage. It means I've got to work at it. I've spoken to a few of my clients about this. They've paid for guys who are truly blessed, who make a big play of being ten- or twelve-inchers, or who have a girth that could plug a manhole. No pun. But that's all they get, and, so they say – because I have this only on second-hand authority – being hammered with a monster member loses its charm after a while. I can imagine. Apparently those are the professionals who go with guys too. Whereas an appreciation of the female form and the type of imagination that you need with an average prick gives you, well, all the incentives that you need. Furthermore, if you're not so blessed in the bungalow department, then, like me, you have to be prepared to do pretty much anything.

Like I said, I like to look after myself and always have done, even before I got into this line of work; I'm not a muscle freak, but I'm not shy of gyms and have been going since I started living in London. It's quality time to spend with yourself, after all.

Self-confidence is also a factor: there's a joke about Argentines that I think illustrates the point. There are two Argentine men in the street. One says to the other, 'Have you got a light?' The other pats his chest, his trouser pockets, and his back pockets. 'No,' he replies. 'But I've got a fantastic body.' I'm not sure where I stand on genes and personalities, but I've never lacked confidence, and an optimistic outlook is very useful in this trade.

I said earlier that I'd come back to body hair. Chest hair some women like, some don't have an opinion. But

11

the female world, as far as I can tell, is united in a remarkably intense dislike for back and shoulder hair, so I remove it.

Depilation has two advantages: firstly, it removes the offensive rug that only bear fetishists and Eastern European wrestlers seem to tolerate. Secondly, it gives you a greater understanding of the dedication that women have to looking good. The first few times I wept like a child after only the first couple of strips. But with practice, whisky and a couple of painkillers beforehand, I got used to the sting. My clients make the effort, and they're paying, so it's the very least I can do.

I've even found work while taking care of the product, as it were; like I said, word of mouth is all-important, and I'm convinced someone's spread the word at the gym. A couple of times I've found myself being checked out there.

On one occasion, a woman in her thirties kept looking at me as if I were familiar. She was dressed in skin-tight gym kit that offered such minimal coverage that it barely passed for underwear, with her dark hair tied severely back in a ponytail. She gave off the air of a marketing manager on her day off, a powerful woman pounding away on the treadmill next to me. As her determined stare caught my eye, it became clear that someone had pointed her in my direction. I smiled back and then later popped a sneaky business card into her gym bag. She duly called a couple of days later and we were soon carrying out a special workout of our very own. I was most impressed by the ease with which she crossed over from her gym routine to her sex life.

The town house where I visited her was glassy and pristine, furnished with low angular surfaces and leather seats. Down a floor was what first looked like a gym:

padded benches, a trapeze, what might have been a vaulting horse. She appeared, wearing a silk kimono, her black hair still tied tightly back. I was in tight jeans and a T-shirt, thinking she would go for the casual look.

'Let's be clear,' she began. 'I've hired you for rough sex.'

'Can't you get that yourself?'

'A lot of men get intimidated. I hope that doesn't happen to you.'

'What if I'm too rough?'

'I don't envisage that being a problem.'

Before I could reply, she was under my guard. Somehow, one leg went around me while her hands pushed my shoulders. I was tipped onto my back, before she straddled me. Under her kimono she was near naked and very firm, and in one moment I was winded and turned rock hard. She grabbed my hands and pinned me down before tearing open my jeans and then the wrapper off a condom that appeared from nowhere. She grabbed my cock like I imagine she grabbed a barbell and jerked herself onto it, pulling aside a micro thing.

In a moment she'd manoeuvred herself just right onto me and in a dozen strokes had me defenceless beneath her, listening to her moaning noisily on top. As I tensed myself, I noticed that the room was not just a gym: it was also a sex room: the vaulting horse had wrist straps, the benches were padded in all the right places. As the sweat of her first orgasm appeared on her brow, I took advantage of a moment's relaxation and kicked myself up.

'Yes!' she screamed as her back hit the mat. I pinned her hands down and then pulled out of her. I hadn't come and was holding myself tight. I slid an arm around her and pulled her to her feet before shoving her towards the vaulting horse. She hit the leather surface with a gasp of pain and joy. I kicked off my trousers and top, and before she had a chance to recover pinned her to the leather with my forearm. I slipped her hands into the straps, met with only faint resistance, and pulled them tight.

'I bet you want me inside you, don't you?' I whispered.

'Yes,' she moaned through gritted teeth.

I kicked her legs apart and then reached down and with two fingers snapped off her thong before opening her soaking lips, and then slid into her, slowly at first, and then with increasing speed and force. She came twice more, screaming and sweating as I pushed her against the leather.

'Now this is what you get for playing rough,' I said. I pulled out of her and stood back. Her legs were apart, her hands were tied at either end of the horse, but she had a wicked look in her eye. I knew what she wanted.

'Go on. Try your best,' she started to hiss. But before she finished the sentence, I vaulted over and pulled back her hair. I peeled off the condom with the other hand. Her mouth shot open with a gasp, and she had little choice but to welcome my cock with open lips. I slid further in as we stared each other in the eye, and I fucked her mouth slow and hard until I came deep down her throat. Once I'd finished, she pulled her hands from the straps and stepped back, admiringly.

'You are a very bad man, Mr Aleixandre,' she said, smirking and wiping her mouth. Before I could come up with a suitable riposte, she had jumped the vault, rugby tackled me, placed her knees on my shoulders and her feet on her hands, her hands on the bar of the trapeze, and, more importantly, the thin strip of her pussy perfectly within tongue's reach. I stretched out my tongue and she lowered herself onto it, before shifting so her clit was on its tip. She was even good enough to show me some gymnastic tricks, including how to turn the splits into the lotus position without letting her clit leave my tongue. Her juices ran down into my mouth, strong and arousing. Two more screaming orgasms later, she pulled herself off and stood over me, eyeing my erection.

'Well. I think we're equal now,' she said.

It took about twenty minutes to go down. Meanwhile, I had the bruises for a week.

Chapter Four

In my work, it helps to live and work where I do: not quite suburban, not quite the heart of town, with a mix of offices, galleries, fancy shops, gyms and parks. Yes, Primrose Hill is a good place for this job. There are few men around during the day and quite a lot of women with time on their hands and money in their Mulberry bags. Occasionally Celeste and I will hang out in cafés there, drinking coffee and, in her case, idly smoking out the door. She always has time to kill, and I enjoy observing the trends and tendencies on the streets of my hometown; I've come to consider it an important area of research for my work: I need to know what the average man of leisure looks like so I can avoid it like the plague.

The only problem with all these luxuries is the cost. When I was a semi-failed jobbing actor, I often found gym fees bouncing straight out of my account. But work now pays for it, and it's become a necessity rather than a luxury. I have to buy a lot of clothes too, as different clients have different needs: some want a rough, denim-y type, others prefer the young city gent, and I am ever eager to please. It was Celeste who suggested that I should try to get these sorts of things as tax deductible. But as I don't really pay any tax on my sex work – shh, don't tell anyone – I guess trying to claim any back would be frankly cheeky.

Despite the cost, there are bonuses to be had spending a lot of time in shops. I've heard a lot of stories from gay friends about their illicit liaisons in the changing rooms at Topman in town. I believe it. Half of the people out shopping aren't just looking for clothes, and commerce seems to get the adrenaline flowing.

I've always liked shop girls, to the point of giving away freebies. One of the local girls has almost become a regular. It started in the early days, soon after I'd started seeing clients. I must have been starting out, sorting out a few outfits for dates, when I found myself in a little boutique by the Hill. It was mid morning, a warm spring day outside, and no one else was shopping. The girl behind the clear glass counter was Italian, with a harshly cut fringe, and a black smock. I must have been looking for jeans. We chatted fairly aimlessly about clothes; she let slip that she was an exchange student, and I got the impression there was more to our chat than professional attention. As I tried things in the changing room, I caught her looking at me in the crack in the curtain. I made some excuse to call her over, and when she went away I left the curtain open some more.

'What do you think about these ones?' I asked, giving her a twirl.

She smiled, giggled to herself, and came back.

'Let me look more closely,' she said, eyeing me up and down.

'Come closer, if you like,' I said. She put a hand on my hip and I drew her towards me, inside the curtain.

'Careful,' she said, 'someone could enter.'

'Yes,' I said, trying not to laugh. 'Someone could.' I put my hands on her hips and lifted her dress over her head. She had small, pert tits with hard nipples. She gave a shiver as I cupped them and kissed her.

'Go quickly,' she said, looking over her shoulder.

'Oh no. You don't want that,' I said.

I guided her round and helped her onto the little leather seat, before kneeling in front of her. I moved the see-through mesh of her knickers to one side and put my tongue to work. I hummed lightly to make my tongue vibrate on her clit, and she came quickly, noisily, with cries and shouts in Italian and other languages I couldn't speak.

'My turn,' I said, standing back up and unzipping the fly of my new jeans. My penis popped out, and she set to licking it along the length. She worked her tongue all over and then swallowed it deep in her mouth.

'Come, now, come on,' she said.

I shook my head, lifted her to her feet.

'Not yet,' I said.

I pulled her knickers down and took out a condom. With it on, I grabbed her buttocks. She reached out and grabbed the coat hook behind me, and I lifted her up and then onto my cock. She rocked herself to another coming before I let myself go, coming deep inside her. She slipped off me, found some clothes, adjusted herself, and stepped unsteadily out of the cubicle.

I tidied myself up, packed up my things in my bag, and stepped out in my new clothes. That was how the deal started: every few weeks I'd pop in when I knew it would be empty, give the little Italian girl something special, and leave with a little something courtesy of her employers, with a little nod and a wink from both of us. It suited the pair of us perfectly.

Chapter Five

I mentioned my friend Celeste, didn't I? It's important in this profession to have good female friends, particularly ones you can discuss things with, and Celeste is a very good one at that. Firstly, she seems to get me a lot of work: friends of hers, employers and once even an older woman who looked a lot like her and who never quite cleared up who she was.

Celeste is also great because of what I can learn from her. Not necessarily because she tells me what women want – I'm not sure she really knows what she wants, in life, let alone from men. No, really, what I learnt from Celeste is what men shouldn't do.

You see, Celeste attracts men in a strange way; not like moths to a flame, although there are a fair few married men who dally with her, write cheques they can't cash and then find themselves scurrying back home after she tires of them and they realise the potential consequences of their straying.

Any man with a functioning libido would be attracted to her – I certainly was, when we met, years ago at some party or another. She wears clothes that border on the bizarre but are also often revealing and provocative. Her haircuts – often featuring masses of dark curls, backcombing and layers – are always cutting edge. She can wear sunglasses that would look utterly ridiculous on anyone else. If it's not her cleavage, then her perfect pins will be obviously displayed. But she seems to achieve all of this as if by accident.

I suspect it's a class thing, or perhaps there's a college somewhere that teaches pouting and insouciance.

Without trying, she picks up men. But despite the obvious attractions, she and I very quickly went into the friend stage, and that was that as far as sex goes. She flirts with me, a lot, but in a half-hearted, teasing way, more for herself than for me, and she seems perfectly comfortable being half-naked around me.

No, Celeste attracts men like crumbs to butter, that's it. Her relationships are strange, and generally short-lived. She accepts offers for dates from relative strangers, and has a series of exes and sort-ofs who, in general, are ignorant of each other's existences. She seldom expresses much enthusiasm for any of them, but sleeps with, well, pretty much all of them.

Once I had her tot up her ongoing relationships, and it reached double figures, but none of them, she insisted, was serious. Most of them had come about through little or no action on her part. There was a newspaper editor she met at a fundraiser her uncle organised, a one-night stand that had turned into something that to most men would have seemed fairly regular. She kept in touch with – literally – two or three old university friends on a quite regular basis.

Then there was a photographer guy she'd started sleeping with after a shoot for a weekend supplement, as well as a make-up guy who almost everyone swore was gay but yet periodically converted for dear Celly. She occasionally mentioned an older man, who picked her up from the flat in a large black Bentley, driven by a white-gloved chauffeur and who had once flown her to his castle in Scotland for a weekend, from which she had returned bored and unimpressed. The others were vague forms, or simply a name and number.

With Celeste and men, it's something that happens as if by magnetism, and the results are seldom pretty to look at. I'll give you a better example. We were sitting in a pub in Camden one afternoon. I was killing time before going to see a local client, she was, well, doing the little that she seems to do to get by. I was leafing through the sports pages, she was drinking gin and tonic and thinking about going for a smoke while prying into my business affairs in a half-mocking way, arching her exquisite eyebrows over one of the infinite pairs of Wayfarers she seems never to take off. I think we must have looked very clearly not like a couple.

On a table across from us there were two thirty-something blokes, day-tripping down to London in short-sleeved shirts and kicker boots. One had a diamond stud earring, the other a scar by his mouth that looked like an ancient glassing injury. They were not, let's be clear, men who should consider themselves Celeste's type. I could see one of them eyeing up Celeste, who smiled periodically, apparently out of politeness. Eventually, one of them came over.

'Mind if we join you?' he asked.

Celeste kind of shrugged. The men came over and sat on two of the chairs at the table. They continued their conversation, trying to engage Celeste in chat. She made polite noises, mostly ignored them and occasionally popped out to smoke. One of the guys accompanied her, but didn't smoke.

Soon, a college friend of Celeste's wandered in, presumably by chance, with another pal of his. They were arty types, in skinny jeans and three-in-one haircuts, doing running and odds-and-sods jobs for a fashion company in town; her friend was showing off a recently acquired neck tattoo. I think Celeste might have slept with one of them, once. He and his pal joined us, while I found myself awkwardly discussing football with the two older men. Mostly, us chaps talked amongst ourselves.

The two older guys got drunker and drunker, offering Celeste drinks that she turned down. Her ex-shag looked embarrassed and over keen. Not long later, another of his friends came over – he'd been sitting at the bar, he may even have worked there – and started trying to chat up Celeste, who was polite and pouty but apparently – or at least it was apparent to me – uninterested.

A few minutes passed before a guy who Celeste was sort of seeing – the photographer I mentioned, a guy in his thirties with a studio round the corner from the pub – wandered in and saw the girl who he took to be his girlfriend – I'm not sure what Celeste thought – surrounded by six men he didn't know. He made as if to call her to one side, but she ignored him with a half pout and a smile. One of the first guys (it had to be the one with the scar) stood up: 'Are you having a go at her?'

'I don't know who you are, but this is my girlfriend. Anyway, what the fuck is it to you?' replied the photographer.

Her college friend stood up and tried to calm things down. It didn't work. I decided that the best spot to observe from was the bar, and slunk away. I bumped into a girl I sort of half-remembered from a job (a legit job, that is) I'd had a while back. She was friendly and flirty, and we exchanged numbers. Just as I thought it might be going somewhere (I had already planned our swift exit route to the gents or, better still, my place), I heard the sound of a pint being thrown, very soon followed by swearing and, inevitably, punches.

Celeste had also snuck away, tiptoeing rather embarrassed but quite quickly away from the scene, and joined me at the bar, scotching my chances with the other girl who immediately took me for both a philanderer and a lightning rod for trouble. Back at the table, a full-scale brawl had erupted, which pitted an unlikely set of combatants and fighting styles against each other, including rather artsy flapping and a camera bag being swung. It was, unsurprisingly, going a lot better for the two short-sleeved thugs than the snapper and the fey student-types. Soon bar staff and a couple of random punters waded in to try and keep the scrappers apart.

'Celeste, look what you've started,' I said, as my potential pick-up walked off.

Celeste gave me a look somewhere between dirty and filthy.

'What? What did I do?'

'Nothing. That's the problem,' I answered with a smirk. 'Except pout, and smile, and be yourself.'

Yes, watching men around Celeste is very often an object lesson in what I shouldn't do, either professionally or for pleasure: drunken schmoozing, leering and letching, not knowing when to leave a girl alone, cheesy chat-up lines, being pushy around other blokes: Celeste attracts the lot. I've even taken to keeping a list of things I see guys do around her, and making a note not to do them myself.

'I'm off,' I said. 'You coming?'

'Yeah,' she said. 'Honestly, Cesc, you have such a strange opinion of me.'

'Think of it as a compliment,' I said, as the police sirens sounded up the Parkway outside.

Next time I'll let you in on some secrets of the trade. It's only fair, after all.

Chapter Six

I got distracted again. Sorry. So, as I was saying, how does it work?

The honest answer is that even now I'm not too sure. I once asked one of my regulars, V., how long she'd been paying for sex. She was a posh divorcée who'd done well in the settlement and then done even better investing the cash in an online sex emporium. Her bedroom – boudoir was probably more appropriate – boasted almost every sex toy or apparatus that could be imagined: three-headed vibrators, ornamental love beads, all sorts of straps, poles and restraints.

But despite having access to toys even I didn't understand that came with paperback-thick instruction manuals, she liked two things and two things only: oral sex, and being fucked hard. On the one hand, she was the simplest job I had. I saw her once a week, and with the vaguest of preludes, I set down to pushing her to orgasm after orgasm, as she kneeled in front of me, her hands tight on the rail of the custom-built bedstead. But she was also the hardest work I had to do, a genuine workout for my thighs. But I shouldn't complain: for all the work my thighs did, my cock had a great time of it.

On this occasion, after she'd finally given in and I'd come, I rolled over and breathed a sigh before asking vaguely, exhausted, with no idea quite where the question came from, how long she'd been paying for sex.

Oddly, she echoed my most cynical pal.

'Always,' she said.

Her rationale for my services was simple. As she

puffed on a cigarette and I lazily stroked her breasts and stomach, she told me a story.

'I'd been happily divorced for about a year, I think. I'd been doing the whole speed dating, Internet dating thing. It was just a waste of time, and the sex was bloody awful.' She flicked her hair off her forehead while I ran my fingers towards her thighs.

'Frankly it was getting me down. I bit the bullet and paid about two hundred pounds for a Coco de Mer vibrator that doubled as an avant-garde ornament. You see it, it's over there,' she said nodding towards one shelf or another. 'It's marvellous, by the way.'

'I know, I think we used it once,' I said.

'Well I've always used them, I've always, you know, masturbated, I mean my husband was a useless sod, so I might as well have something that looks good. But the casual sex I was getting was terrible, and I really didn't need to be tied down. Men only seem to have the confidence to fuck when they're drunk, and then they're generally poor.'

'It's a real pity they can't make booze that improves potency, eh.'

'Yes. So I figured, why not combine the two.'

'The two what?' I answered, not quite getting the gist as I began to kiss her neck.

'The dating and the expense.'

'Ahhh. So I'm basically a walking vibrator.'

'I don't need you to walk,' she retorted.

'Why, do I get a rest now?'

'Sort of,' she said, pushing my head towards her pussy.

I smiled. She was right, I thought, as I tongued towards her sex.

Apart from her, why are so many women willing to

25

pay for sex? And when I say 'so many', I'll admit that's something of a guess. The numbers are tricky to work out. I can't believe that I'm the only guy offering this sort of service. I've looked in magazines, and there are plenty of adverts, although not of course as many as there are for women offering the same thing. There's not a union, as far as I know, so quite how you'd work it out, I don't know. Asking women is probably not the best way.

I only need about fifteen or so regulars on top of what could be called passing trade to keep me in pretty good style. So how many women are at it? I don't know. Some no doubt have more than one regular paid screw. I see most of my regulars weekly or fortnightly, and I'm sure most women would want more sex than that a week. So the numbers must be significant.

I've even been hired by third parties. One of my favourite assignments was as a personal trainer. Of a very special type. A new husband's mother hired me to help 'train' his young wife. They do talk about 'helicopter parents', don't they? Without her son knowing, the mother contacted me and paid me to go through a few tricks with her daughter-in-law, in the interest of her son's ongoing happiness. I was happy to teach her some tricks, but I'll be honest: it really didn't take much to get her out of herself, and soon she was coming up with ideas even more exciting and elaborate than those on my list.

Going back to the question then: I think so many women are willing to pay for sex because bad sex is so easy to come by. Hell, I've been responsible for giving bad sex myself, although certainly not in a professional capacity: drunken fumbles at student parties; the time I fell off a girlfriend and her bed, broke two fingers in the fall and had to spend the night in casualty instead of in her; or with the girl with a strange complex who would only let me put the tip in.

You see, women can get bad sex in so many places: with boyfriends who are more interested in the football; with husbands who are fat and dull; with drunk guys you pick up in bars; and with Internet dates who bore you near to tears.

That's not to say that any of these don't have their advantages, and I'm sure plenty of women make do. But if you're after pure, unadulterated, guilt-free, good sex, well, there are few places where it's guaranteed. Which, as you've guessed, is where I come in.

I've asked Cel about this; we have some pretty frank conversations. I asked her to estimate how many times she came, on average, with a guy: the figure was a small fraction of the men she'd slept with, and an even smaller fraction of the shags she'd ever had.

'That must be very disappointing,' I said.

She sort of pouted.

'I guess. Sometimes I'm not even sure why I bother.'

'That's a sad situation, Celeste,' I said. 'No wonder you have calluses on your hands.'

She poked me, hard under the ribs.

'There's no need for that. If you were half a man you'd fuck me as a favour,' she teased.

'You couldn't afford me, Cel dear.'

OK, enough about bad sex. Next time we'll talk practicalities.

Chapter Seven

So, like I said, the practicalities.

I don't, and never have, tried that hard to get clients. Most of them come to me by word of mouth. I guess that girls must talk, and at least half of my regulars seem to know each other, or at least that's the impression I get.

In the first few months, clients seemed to proliferate like an outbreak of flu. A friend of mine who had a job in marketing explained it. You have early adopters, in this case women who know the game and are prepared to try out a new guy who they've heard is available. Then you get the second wave, who've either had a recommendation or are a bit unsure about the whole thing and wait until they know that either the set-up or the guy is kosher. Then things settle down, and you have a solid set of regulars, with occasional additions and occasional fall-offs. Surprisingly, marriage tends to lead to a hiatus, rather than a full cancellation. And on top of that, I guess there's what you might call passing trade and casual enquiries.

Then there are the business cards. I give my regulars a few to pass on. I've always trusted them to do this, guessing that it would be a very short-sighted Jenny who would get possessive about a call guy.

Celeste is normally good enough to pass on my details to agents, managers, photographers and other wealthy bohemian types who like what I have to offer. She's one of my best sources of custom, but as I'm the only one of us who really works, it's the least she can do. I also have a couple of Internet posts. In fact it was an early and very generous regular who advised me of a couple of websites that specialise in erotica, fiction, and contacts for ladies in the know.

I also have a phone number just for the purpose: a discreet mobile that I answer only occasionally. There's nothing more tacky than people with too many phones, answering them all the time in public. It also makes you look like you're selling something that's not sex. A message will do as I always call back. Rates are generally agreed in advance, as are the details of the assignment, whether it's an evening session, a date, or a whole night (rare, as I said). Celeste helped me work out the fees – I was far too cheap at first, and eventually I decided that the hourly rate should come down with time spent.

I make no demands of clients, other than they pay up and tell me plainly what they want, or at least allow me to guess and don't get too shirty if I guess wrong. After a few months it began to become pretty much obvious what each client, be she regular or new girl, wanted. Sometimes it's the glint in the eye that suggests sexual gymnastics or the steely gaze of the primly dressed miss who wants to be blindfolded and tied while I insult the memory of her mother.

And unless it's illegal, or seriously dangerous, I never say no. I have turned down some things: one woman wanted me to break into her house, masked and menacing, and ravish her by force. It sounded a bit dark to me, but that wasn't a problem, in itself. I even looked into sourcing a crowbar and balaclava.

The problem arose when I insisted on using a safe word (it's something I'd read about on a bondage site): a word she could say that couldn't occur in the course of the little set-up, but that would tell me that a line had been crossed. I suggested 'safe', which she rejected as too, well, 'safe'; 'no', which she rejected because she said it was an important part of the game, and then 'chicken', which she thought could easily be used as an insult and might quite naturally be uttered. Eventually, I sacked her off as a timewaster and hung up.

Sometimes I can get a surprise, like the small, quietly spoken art teacher who shared a flat with her sister and hired me because she wanted to try out a strap-on on a guy. Hey, I said I never say no, although it was a strange experience, I'll confess.

She let me go on 'top' first; I turned her round and pinned her hands down over her head. Meanwhile I fucked her steadily while playing with her clit, bringing her to two trembling orgasms. Then the strange stuff started: she stepped away from the bed and rummaged around in a drawer that looked like it should hold sheet music or primary school marking; instead, she emerged with what looked like a leather jockstrap with a black penis attached.

'This might hurt,' she said, as I assumed the position. She was right, but it was bearable. And she was paying. After a while of being rogered, as she panted behind me, I wondered quite where it was leading.

'How about you be a good girl and give a guy a reach-around?' I asked. I winced after a particular vehement stroke, but soon she had her hand on my cock. Her little hand made it look even bigger as she wanked me off over the bed. After a while I even got used to the sensation of having her in me, and I came, hard and hot into her hand.

'Next time,' I said, 'you're going to find out what that's like.'

And she did: I think she liked it a lot more than I did.

There aren't really many other rules. I expect

payment in cash in advance, even with my regulars. It keeps things a lot simpler and makes it clear precisely what the deal is. I'll wear what you like, and you can do likewise; I'm not fussy, and indeed why would I be? If we're out in public, it's best not to mention precisely what the circumstances are, mainly because someone told me that it's strictly illegal, although it would be odd to end up in jail for it. Also, quite a few of the nicer restaurants are a bit sniffy about what they know goes on. Come on though. How many of those beautiful exotic girls you see with slightly puffy older gentlemen in hotel bars and restaurants are not in it for money? Why do you think they call it going out for nosh? Well the same goes for me, yet I suppose such establishments must at least keep up appearances.

What else is there? I don't see my clients except on a professional basis and I won't turn tricks for friends as that really does blur the line. Drunkenly Celeste tried to buy head from me once – I'm not sure why, but I suspect that she was teasing as much as anything – and I was quite within my rights to tell her to go screw herself, which I think she probably did judging from the moans, whimpers and faint vibrating sound coming from her room later on. I guess Celeste's problem is probably bad sex and I get the impression she fucks to kill time and masturbates for pleasure. She never seems to talk about her sex life in enthusiastic terms, yet takes a lot of interest in my efforts.

So I suppose the answer is: it just works. Now next time I'll tell you a bit about how I got into this game.

Chapter Eight

It was a bad week when I started on the road towards my current career. I'd been working at a friend's company, a dot-com outfit selling knockdown fashions. The boss was an old school friend of mine whose family worked in fabrics or something similar; I think his granddad had owned a factory somewhere in the Midlands. His dad had decided to expand the business and bought a factory in China that made lookalike clothes and Junior had set up an Internet site that sold these.

Things were going well and they'd moved to a new office off Farringdon Road in one of those new glass-fronted buildings. I think he owed me a favour at the time; I'm not sure why he would have decided to offer me a job otherwise. In fact he called me just after another of my failed auditions and at a weak moment; otherwise I probably wouldn't have accepted. But the idea of a regular wage and something approaching a real job was strangely appealing for someone who was decidedly failing to make it in the media or in showbiz. Apparently, he was having grand designs for world domination. I should have realised then that it was a bad idea even then.

The scheme my pal had hatched to up his sales was to get his slightly ropey wares into big department stores. Simple, he thought: everyone wants a bargain, and concessions were money for nothing.

It was my job to charm buyers from these department stores. The charm I could do at the drop of a trilby; first off, I got myself a date with a girl from men's fashions at Selfridges. She couldn't have been much more than twenty, and I suspected that she might have got the job because of who she knew. Later, after we'd enjoyed a particularly boozy evening at a little vodka bar behind Oxford Street, we found ourselves back at her place, a penthouse overlooking Regent's Park, and I decided that it was either that, or because of her skills in the sack.

After scarcely touching a coffee on her very striking orange leather sofa she was soon sitting on my lap, kissing me as we undressed each other. She gave me a spectacular blow job as I enjoyed the view through the floor-to-ceiling window, more importantly with her perfect butt reflected in it. Just before I was going to come, I stopped her and perched her back on my lap. She slipped my cock inside her and rocked her way to an orgasm that shook us off the sofa and onto the thick tiger-skin rug. I didn't let the radical chic of the design put me off. I made her turn around and I slid deeper inside her; she moaned appreciatively, hooking her ankles over mine to lock us together. Twice more she moaned loudly to climax, before I let myself go and came deep inside her. As I pulled out, the condom was soaked in her juices.

But despite my best efforts, there was no sale.

A few weeks later, I got chatting at length to a buyer from Liberty. She was tall and slim, in her forties I guess, and specialised in fancy fabrics. Work-wise, I hadn't a hope – Liberty weren't going to touch my mate's wares with a finely wrought obsidian and jet barge pole. But I clocked the absence of a wedding ring and the dallying conversation that strayed on to lighter matters than next year's stock patterns. I invited her for a coffee, and with no great effort persuaded her to knock off early that afternoon. At some stage she'd mentioned a particular design feature of her flat, which I agreed to let her show me.

On that very skinny pretence we found ourselves at her place, half a town house in Mayfair, where we spent a wholly pleasurable afternoon fucking each other's brains out. I particularly remember doing my bit for the field of fabrics and drapery, as we put her baroque-pattern silk curtain ties to a far more pleasurable use, after she asked to be tied and blindfolded as I tongued her to orgasm.

But again, great sex, no sale. Indeed, no one was buying our wares, regardless of whether I was having sex with her or not. Sadly – and I say this very much with hindsight, as at the time it seemed the most sensible thing in the world – that didn't seem to stop the business forking out vast sums. They paid for new furniture, away days, wild expenses and graphic designers. Around me colleagues were turning up in a new suit and a different watch every day. For my part, I helped myself to any number of freebies and charged pretty much every breath, bite and movement to the company, including several quite spectacularly successful dates. So even then, I guess, I was being paid to fuck.

The final straw for the business came in October: a bunch of kids broke into the warehouse we had just off the M25. While trying to smoke a few spliffs and muck around with their scooters, they managed to set fire to a whole season and a half's worth of stock. Apparently my pal didn't have quite as much business acumen as he'd made out, and insurance had been beyond his imagination. With no stock and thousands of pounds worth of orders outstanding, the business folded.

I'd been there two months: I'd turned down auditions and even some modelling work. I was *persona non grata* with all my previous contacts. As is the fate of most out-of-work jobbing actors-cum-models, I ended up in behind my local bar, back in Chalk Farm.

Chapter Nine

Bar work had its advantages, though, at least for a while. I slept in late, I ate for free, I met lots of people.

But there was one quite specific advantage that I should mention.

Barmaids.

Barmaids are, of course, a long-standing sexual cliché: busty German wenches serving Bavarian brew to lusty males; wholesome farmers' daughters bunking up with Chaucerian students. Most men have one fond memory or another from their youth of a favourite barmaid.

Nowadays, the key with barmaids is to get them when they've just arrived. The psychological and physical effects of working behind a bar are not attractive. Girls whose work includes spending large chunks of the day snacking on bar food and crisps, and most of the evening supping beer, end up flabby and bored very soon. Although bored women are fair game, they've got to at least show an interest and be worth the hard yards.

Meanwhile, in their defence, the experience of being leered at by sweating drunks makes them quite rightly wary about men as a species. But newly arrived barmaids, as well as tending to be the very cream of the student, actress, wannabe-model crowd, are generally looking to make friends. There are a lot of people in London desperate to make friends. Barmaids have at least gone a step further and taken a job that makes it easy. And furthermore, most of them are up for casual and often rather quite adventurous sex.

After a week I'd managed two quickies in the cellar

with a little Danish blonde who was in town to perfect her already excellent English. She also seemed to revel in what most would have considered quite uncomfortable positions. I can't quite remember how it got started. I expect the landlord, a cheery old Welshman who spent almost no time in the pub he was meant to run and an awful lot of time boozing the profits away in one mate's premises or another, decided to let me show her the ropes. I suppose it was his idea of a favour for holding the fort while he disappeared for the evening.

We were busy and a pump ran dry. The girl asked me if I'd show her how to change it. I nodded to the other guy on and went downstairs with her.

In the cellar I realised that I had walked into something from a Carry On film. Not only was it extremely hot, but we were in a room full of pumps and hoses. I tried to avoid one horrible pun or another as I explained to her how to unhook the line and reconnect with a new barrel. I saw her looking attentively at me and carried on biting my tongue. After the demonstration, I asked if she knew what to do.

'I bet you're thinking this is like some kind of porno,' she said, to my complete surprise.

'I'm sorry?' I managed to blurt.

'You, a little blonde girl. In the cellar full of pumps.'

'Right. I hadn't really thought of it like that,' I said, lying.

'Or Carry On.'

'How do you know about Carry On films?'

'I'm here to learn English, right.'

'By watching Carry On films?'

'Yes. Look, I know what you're thinking.'

'I'm thinking we should probably get back upstairs before they think something's up.'

'Yeah right,' she said. 'I think it already is. Come on, do you think we have time?'

'For what … oh, right.' I checked my watch. 'Well I've always got time to brush up on a little Danish,' I said, almost cringing myself. She laughed, and reached out. We kissed, only briefly, before she went for my fly. Meanwhile I hitched up her pinny and tore her tight black trousers down to her ankles.

'This might be uncomfortable,' I said, as I turned her round and bent her towards a barrel. She laughed again, while I slipped her G-string down from her perfect buttocks. The first time was brief, but she enjoyed being fucked like that enough to make another more or less laughable excuse to invite me down there later that evening, and by the end of the week I'd managed to screw her several ways over a barrel, with our heads squeezed under the low ceiling and her attempting to come without letting her gritted-teeth shouts reach either the staff room or the bar upstairs. I've always loved an adventuress, particularly one with as flexible a little frame as she had.

At the same time I'd also been getting on very well with the assistant manageress, a sharp-eyed American girl financing an MBA somewhere in the city. She clearly didn't need the money, as her flat over the canal suggested that someone with a lot of spare cash was bankrolling the whole deal. She and the landlord made the unlikeliest of professional pairings, but it seemed to work. She came up with one bright idea after another to bring in the punters and the cash, while he boozed it away and let her have run of the place.

Alongside the MBA and the bar work, she'd obviously decided to let rip with a set of fantastic perversions that she had brought with her from across the water. We had our first encounter one evening, later after a shift, as we sat on the sofa in the pub waiting for the boss to return. She was chilly and professional with me at first, but relaxed after a couple of VTs, and soon we were chatting like old friends. I invited her to continue the fun at my place, once the boss was back, but she insisted on showing me her flat. We made love that evening, pretty much standard vanilla milkshake stuff, but the second time round there she began to unleash. Firstly, she had me tie her up with a long leather strap. The second time, she produced a metal bar with two ankle loops, which she had me secure her in before I fucked her with her ankles spread wide over her head.

The next time, she told me we needed to step up a gear. I tied her fully this time – ankles on the bar, hands tightly tied to the bedposts, before gagging her and beating her buttocks with what I can only describe as a paddle, before I finally got to fuck her.

The next time, she produced candles: once she was tied, the wax had to be picked off, soft and applied to her nipples; once it dried, it was to be torn off. Then the same on her pussy. I wasn't wholly convinced, but it got her sopping wet before I screwed her. For the second round, it was to be dripped on, slowly, with her hands and feet bound to the corners of the bed. I was fairly sure that this would cause damage, but even then I was never one to turn down a reasonable offer.

She was, at least, even handed. Over the week, for each of the several occasions on which she demanded to be spanked, tied or penetrated in unusual fashion, I was equally beaten, whipped and singed. The candles that filled her flat were not just for adornment; nor was the riding crop. I can't say I was as keen on the pain as she was, but as a means to an end it suited me fine. I guess we both got different things out of it: if dirty bondage games got me into a dripping wet, welcoming pussy, all the better. Meanwhile, I think she used the sex to talk me into more and more surprising little tricks. Only when I found myself at work with a customer enquiring as to whether a cat had scratched my neck and then another asking whether the pub had a H&S policy for burns did I realise that perhaps things needed calming down a little.

Chapter Ten

Then there was the other advantage: the customers.

The combination of office girls working in largely female environments and gallons of white wine has always been an explosive mixture. As a single barman, it's hard not to take advantage. I'd had a word with one of the bouncers, and occasionally I'd find myself in the secluded little alley out the back having guiltless fun with one customer or another while he sneakily looked on. As well as being harmless, the sex was often effortless. I think drunk girls see oral as some sort of safety measure. On a couple of occasions it took little more than a brief exchange of words to find myself throat deep in an account handler or sales exec. Occasionally, after an early shift, I'd knock off at six to, well, knock off with the same girl; after all, it's rude not to return favours.

It was Celeste who suggested that I might have an addiction.

'How many girls have you had sex with in the last month?' she asked me. She was propping up the bar, considering a cigarette, while I lazily wiped a glass and eyed up the female half of a business deal who looked like a distinct possibility. Celeste and I had shared a flat for a year or so, after she'd fallen out with an old school chum who wanted to move a boyfriend in, and I'd decided I no longer wanted to share a house with six other people and only one bathroom.

'Are you jealous? We could share,' I said to her.

'No. Moron,' she sneered. 'But seriously. You don't know, do you?'

I thought briefly. 'Ten maybe. Fifteen? Possibly.'

'Shit. Cesc, that's ridiculous.'

'It's been a good month. You know the joke, right?'

'Joke?'

'What's the difference between a car tyre and thirty used condoms?'

'I don't know,' she said, trying not to look like she cared.

'One's a Goodyear, one's a good month.'

'Ha ha,' she said, without a smile. 'Seriously, though. It's a lot.'

'Maybe. By the way, are we counting head?'

'Yes.'

'But eating's not cheating.'

'You don't have anyone to cheat on. And it's still eating,' she added vaguely stirring her Tanq' and tonic.

'Anyway, shut up. Someone will hear. I'd hate to give the wrong impression.'

'You idiot. Anyway,' she continued, fiddling with her unnecessary indoor shades, 'you've got a problem.'

'It would only be a problem if I couldn't get any. I don't even think there's such a thing as sex addiction. An addiction would be your smoking. I'm sure your smoking is a comforter. Did your first boyfriend have a really small, two-tone dick? With a Marlboro tattoo up the side?'

'Screw you.'

'You know it's bad for your health. Maybe if you didn't smoke you'd have better sex.'

'I'd rather go into a convent than give up.'

'You see, Celeste, you're the one with the addiction. What would you do if they banned it properly?'

'I'd still smoke,' she said, determinedly.

'You'll be fined, you know. Or jailed. You know,

41

Celeste, I'd like to see a pretty girl like you in a women's jail.'

She stuck her tongue out at me.

'That's a real long tongue you got. You're gonna need it where you're going.'

'Piss off,' she said.

'Seriously though, what about the fine? It's a lot of money.'

'I'd smoke if the punishment was death. I'd rather die than quit,' she said, now annoyed at me.

I grabbed her cigarettes and made to throw them into the sink.

'Hey!' she said, grabbing my wrist.

'See. That's an addiction.'

'I could quit if I wanted.'

'Celeste, you just said that you'd rather die than quit.'

'Rather die than have them make me quit, I said. I could quit if I wanted to.'

I broke off a second to serve a customer, an older guy, a big Irish builder off the site, who looked over towards Celeste as if he were about to make a come-on.

'Don't bother, mate,' I said.

'What?' he asked.

'She's,' I whispered across the bar, 'how can I say this. She's a woman in comfortable shoes, you know.'

'Oh. I see.'

He sipped his beer and rubbed some brick dust off his black coat. After a moment he moved along the bar and looked at Celeste.

''Tis a waste, my dear. What you wanna go muff rubbing when there's good cock in the world.'

'I'm sorry?' said Celeste, bewildered, while I tried to contain my laughter. Before she could berate him, the man had turned away, shaking his head, and had sat down with his pint across the other side of the pub.

'Cesc, what the fuck was that about?'

'Who knows, Cel, who knows.'

'I'm going for a cigarette,' she said, flustered.

'See,' I said. 'An addiction. This,' I said, looking at the customer who'd been eyeing me up, 'is simply good luck.'

Chapter Eleven

The luck couldn't last, of course.

It was a Friday night in the bar. I should have realised that something was up when the regular bouncer didn't show. As it was, we were too busy to take too much notice. Paydays were always crazy. Even with direct debits and credit cards, there still seemed to be something about the end of the month that led to wild collective festivities.

The media firm from around the corner was also celebrating something and had block-booked the sofas by the window. I had no idea whether it was a leaving do or a birthday; I didn't pay too much attention to the cards on the table, but I did notice the attentions of the birthday or leaving girl. Her colleagues were egging her on to come to the bar and find fairly pointless excuses to shoot the breeze with me, while buying swimming-pool quantities of booze for herself, her friends and half the bar. She was tall and slender, freckled, neatly dressed and generous with her tips.

We flirted fairly aimlessly as I collected glasses and her friends and colleagues nudged and prodded in schoolgirl fashion. I'm used to this sort of thing; I suppose it comes firstly with the looks, if you'll excuse the vanity, and secondly with the type of work I do. Barmen are fairly neutral, for flirting or something more. Often we're called upon to put pressure on the real object of attentions, which is fine by me. I've no problem helping stir listless men to action provided no jealous boyfriends come looking for a scrap.

After she'd pushed her way assertively through the

scrum at the bar she bought me another drink, which I totted up behind the counter. Then, after a fairly meaningless exchange, she flicked her light red hair behind her ear and pouted tipsily and suggestively. I nodded in the direction of the fire exit and snuck out around the front of the bar. I cast the bouncer a wink, while a couple of my colleagues asked where I was going.

'I'm just checking on the disabled toilets. Apparently there's a problem with the taps.'

It was a fairly standard and believable excuse, or so I thought. Once I was out of sight, the other side of the mêlée at the bar, I ducked through the fire door, left it open, and waited a second as she followed me. It was dark outside, the bins blocking the view from the road.

I leant against the wall and waited.

'So aren't you going to introduce yourself?' she asked.

'I'm Cesc.'

'Che …'

'No.'

'Ke …'

'Still no.'

'Fuck it,' she concluded, walking towards me and grabbing my T-shirt. Dutch courage, clearly. 'I'm really not fussed what you're called.'

She kissed me, drunkenly and lustily. I grabbed her buttocks and pulled her towards me.

'We'll have to be quick. They're expecting me in the disabled toilets.'

She pulled away momentarily and gave me a skewed smile.

'Whatever,' she said, putting her hand on my crotch. 'Come on then.'

I pushed my hands up along her thighs and found, to my pleasant surprise, the side ties of her knickers. Two quick jerks and they were off, revealing a perfectly shaved, silky smooth peach beneath. She was obviously well prepared. She undid my fly and reached for my cock. While I played with her with one hand and she massaged me even harder, I pulled out a trusty Trojan from the wallet in my back pocket. She took it from me, opened it, put the teat between her teeth, and bent over to perform a cunning trick that I love, rolling it down my shaft with the roll against her teeth as my cock moved to the back of her pretty little mouth.

Then she stood up suddenly.

'From behind,' she demanded, moving past me toward the wall.

I followed her round and reached between her legs, pushing her skirt up over her buttocks, spreading her thighs apart and then pushing my cock up and into her. She gasped as I thrust my way further in. She pressed her hands and face against the wall while I held her hips steady with both hands, settling into a steady rhythm. Then I reached round and found her clit, using her moisture to run my index finger up and down it. She came surprisingly quickly, clearly aware of the need for haste, and despite her trembling I managed to control myself, before moving my hands back to her hips to concentrate on my own pleasure.

At which stage, sadly, the door opened. The movement caught my eye, but not hers.

It was my deputy manageress. For a moment I wondered whether she might want to join in and prepared to hold on for a while.

I stopped and the red-haired girl turned too.

'What the …' she began.

46

'I'm sorry missy, but fucking the staff is not included with the price of a drink. Even as much as you had.' The girl as good as jumped off me, a horrified look on her face, before hitching her skirt back down. She shook herself down like a riled cat, before huffing her way back inside the bar. I realised that her knickers were tucked into my pocket and briefly thought about offering to return them.

'And as for you,' added my deputy boss. 'You're fired. Put your fucking cock away and get out.'

'Are you sure I can't put it to some good use? It's like a rock …'

'You disgust me. Get out.'

'You can't fire me. You're not the landlord.'

'If I say you're fired, you're fired. Now get the fuck out.'

Shit. I thought. Sacked, and I hadn't even come.

I also realised that I'd been stitched up. The new bouncer, as well as being a giant who could barely walk because of his muscle-pumped frame, was also a born-again moralist of one strict religion or another. He saw part of his work as a doorman as making sure as little surreptitious sex took place as possible, starting with me. If only I'd realised that it wasn't my usual mate I would have left off the wink and probably gotten away with it.

That evening was the start of a bad run of luck. It's not fun being out of work, particularly when your last two references have gone up in smoke, in one case quite spectacularly, with me doing my best impression of a randy penguin.

Celeste saw it as proof of my addiction. Apparently, once a repetitive habit affects your work, that's a sign of addiction.

'Crap,' I said, but it had started to get under my skin.

Chapter Twelve

In the end, it was clear that it wasn't an addiction.

I think there's a difference between, let's say, crack, and sex. You can steal enough money to get crack, or you can go on a programme, or you can get worse, cheaper drugs. I'm not sure there are drugs that are much worse than crack, but there must be, a bit like when the Costco on my street was undercut by a worse, cheaper all-night beer and crisps store across the way. Anyway, somehow or another, if you're addicted, you'll get high. Maybe that's what happens with proper sex addiction: you end up doing anything with anyone.

But it became pretty clear I didn't have an addiction. I was just trying to get the type of sex I'd been having before and I wasn't getting any. My standards, which have always been broad, I'll admit, didn't shift. I didn't start having sex with monkeys or goats.

It's funny how luck works. I'd lost my job in the bar and with it – I don't know how – my ability to pick up women. I suppose I couldn't tell you how I learnt how to pick up women in the first place. I've been doing it as long as I can remember, often without really trying too hard. I felt like a man who'd woken up one morning and forgotten how to walk. Something that had always come naturally had been turned off like a tap.

I can't help but feel that my job situation was a factor. Being out of work knocks your confidence, and women can spot a guy lacking confidence from a long way off. I'm not lucky enough to have any rich benefactors or family money to fall back on, either, so it wasn't like I could suddenly turn into a man of leisure. When your form is down, you start to try too hard, and like I said, one of the things that I'd learnt from Celeste was that a lot of women steer clear of a pushy guy.

I looked for work in a few other bars, but my ex-manageress had a vindictive streak and had decided to take her revenge by not only sacking me but also letting everyone else in the local trade know that I was a till-sifting punter-botherer. It was particularly upsetting as only half of it was even remotely true. I guess she must have thought that muddying my reputation was a means to ensure that no one would believe any gossip I happened to let slip about her. She obviously doesn't know me well enough. I've never been in the habit of kissing – or screwing, or flogging, or scalding for that matter – and telling.

In the end, as my cash ran dry and one lead after another led nowhere, I was left with no option but the jobcentre.

I'm glad that there isn't an equivalent for people who can't find sex: the North Camden jobcentre is like a cross between the queue at Heathrow airport and a school hall being used to house hurricane victims. The members of staff working in the place want to be there even less than the jobless, particularly my 'case manager', a kid who was my age but looked like a teenager, and who urgently needed someone to tell him to blow his nose instead of constantly sniffling. On one occasion I even suggested to him that we could all solve our problems by swapping sides of the desk. I don't think he got the joke.

None of the staff there could pronounce my name, or understand why I didn't have a funny accent, or indeed what it was I'd ever done with my life. So after two weeks I found myself still on the dole and up against it.

49

It was also a frustrating place for a man on a bad run of luck for another reason: the women. If the staff there are the greyest, least-inspired collection of time-servers you've ever met, they contrast with the great number of extremely sexy, recently arrived Polish, Russian, Bulgarian and God knows where else from young women. All were fresh-faced, ready to impress, and desperate to improve their English by any means necessary.

When I saw the pale, lispy young man who'd failed again to get me a job being greeted by the passionate kiss of Amaja, a gypsy goddess with gravity-defying breasts who I'd seen job seeking only a week before, I realised that the world had gone wrong.

Chapter Thirteen

With no job and no sex, I tried to be creative.

Where do you go to find women and that's free? Correct: galleries and museums.

Galleries and museums are great places: the hushed, reverent silence, the slow movement of visitors. Only libraries have more sexual tension, and talking is forbidden there.

So I started spending a lot of time at the Tate, the South Bank and the Barbican. Different women frequented each one: tourists and language students at the Tate, professionals and arty types by the River and bohemians at the Barbican.

In the past, these had been great spots for quirky, impromptu liaisons, and I'd always loved arty girls. My fondest memory was one visit to the Tate. Upstairs there was some installation or similar, part of a retrospective of one artist or another, whose work consisted of a series of large rectangular mattresses, scattered apparently at random in a big white room.

I wandered around, trying to work out what it was all about, before I caught sight of a pretty little Japanese girl across the way. We sort of half knew each other, as it happened that she'd been dating my friend Archie for a while. I tried not to imagine what horrible perversions he might have subjected her to during their brief liaison.

She was smiling, at the exhibit, at other visitors and at me. Eventually I made my way over to her side of the room.

'Hi Cesc,' she said, with a broad smile.

'Do you understand this?' I asked.

She shook her head.

'No. It's a big bed,' she said, with a giggle.

I looked around to see how full the room was. The member of staff was not on the stool by the wall; a couple of other visitors were vaguely reading the explanatory plaques. I noticed that in one corner of the room, a few of the mattresses had been piled up, making a sort of den.

'Come on,' I said to her. She shot a glance either side, laughed, and we dived towards the corner. Once we were half hidden, I pulled another mattress across the opening and we hid down out of view.

I looked her up and down: she was small, pretty and trendily dressed, in a puffball skirt, a top with rips across it and punky boots. Her hair had been cut into a jagged bob. We kissed, quickly, before she pulled back and looked at me.

'Is this part of the show?' she said, laughing.

'Oh yes. It comes with the donation.'

We kissed again, keeping low to the floor. I ran my hand up her shirt; she was braless and her nipples were hard and stuck out almost further than her tits. My other hand went to her knickers, and she gasped as I slipped my hand under the thin fabric and towards her clit. Soon I had slipped the knickers aside, unzipped my fly and manoeuvred myself between her legs.

'Wow,' she said. I stopped, my cock paused before her pussy.

'What?' I said.

'I love this museum.' I slid into her, slowly, trying not to disturb our shelter. Soon, the sensation took me over. She was hot and tight, and squirmed and whimpered with pleasure beneath me. Soon, we were both coming, breathily and enthusiastically. So enthusiastically, as it happens, that I realised only after I'd rolled away that two or three other punters had been watching the whole scene.

I guess that's the great thing about galleries: people think you're an exhibit. What was it Archie said to me once? A quote from one philosopher or another: 'Art is the ever broken promise of happiness.'

'Of a penis,' I had said to him.

But now, though, sex in museums was just a happy and arousing memory. I was cruising round the same spots, finding only couples and school trips. The few singletons I did see wanted nothing to do with me, I guess suspecting me of being some sort of museum pervert or scammer.

Chapter Fourteen

A month passed: no sex, no job, two more unsuccessful meetings with someone so utterly unlikely to get me a job that he almost laughed at his own efforts, and a lot of frustration watching other people succeeding at what used to be easy for me.

Something had to change, and I decided that if it wasn't the work, then it would start with the sex. And I suppose, inadvertently, it was Celeste's fault that I ended up as a call guy.

This much was Celeste's idea: I started Internet dating.

I seldom take her suggestions too seriously, but this one seemed less feather-brained than usual. She'd been single for a while, once, she told me, and had tried it. Apparently all the guys she met were freaks, losers or frankly frightening. This, she told me in her rather downbeat way, was highly representative of the quality of men in London. That was why she wanted to move to Cuba, or Brazil, where, she insisted, poverty and good weather created the type of man that she wanted. I called her a sex-tourist and she shrugged. I called her a colonialist and she looked at me blankly.

But she had a point: with the gender imbalance, the unacceptability of much of the male population of the city, and with the pressure on women to look and act the part, it can be an easy ride being a guy. Especially in a field like dating.

That afternoon I joined a couple of free Internet dating sites. I noticed that on a number, membership was free for men but at a price for women. This immediately suggested something to me that I had for a long time suspected: a good man is a valuable commodity in this city. Let's be honest, even a passable man can be tricky.

I registered myself as a 'fun member' – I liked the pun – that's to say not someone who is immediately looking for a marriage partner for a booked and arranged wedding within the next six months. Within two hours I had my first message. By the evening, I had a date.

The girl in question claimed to be twenty-four: she'd moved to London after university, split up with her long-term boyfriend and decided that she wanted to have some, you've guessed, 'fun'. After a couple of emails we chatted online and agreed to meet in a pub in Camden that we both knew. I booked a table for dinner, for later. I borrowed some cash from Celeste, who'd been seeing an older gentleman and seemed suddenly to be even more flush than usual. I dressed up and then dressed down, and headed down to meet her.

The girl didn't spot me at first – I'd been perfectly honest about my description – but I recognised her immediately from the photo: slim, very short brown hair, almost boyish figure, casually well dressed in a media-type way. After I waved a few times she seemed to get the hint. Later she admitted that she was shy about wearing her glasses on dates. I called her over and we exchanged a polite kiss before some amiable chat. After she'd had a couple of gin and tonics, I plucked up the courage to ask whether she was a regular Internet dater.

'Can I be honest with you?'

'I hope so.'

'I was in a relationship with one guy for seven years. He left me. He'd been sleeping around behind my back. A lot. That included a good friend of mine and a girl I used to sit next to at work.'

'Ouch,' I said.

'He was a wanker. And I realised that life's just too short. I wanted some variety before I settled down.'

I contained the urge to laugh with glee before nodding understandingly.

'OK. Well, do you really want to go for dinner?'

She laughed, slightly nervously, before responding with a smile.

'No. I live round the corner. Shall we go?'

I didn't bother to finish my drink. We barely spoke during the five-minute walk. She looked at me, smiling cheekily, a couple of times. A minute or so away from her door, she held my hand.

As soon as we were inside the door, she stepped up on tiptoes to kiss me, passionately and clumsily. The height difference made us stumble across the hall towards the narrow staircase – she lived on the first floor of a Camden terrace – and we found ourselves kissing and grappling with each other's clothes, half on the floor, half on the stairs. I half pushed her top up to reveal small breasts with bullet nipples – no bra. As I slid my hand up her skirt and between her legs, I found she had no underwear.

'My kind of girl,' I said.

'My kind of boy,' she replied, pulling my stiff cock from out of my jeans.

'The neighbours?' I asked.

'They're out.'

I fumbled a condom out of my wallet and slipped it on before hitching her skirt up. The time out of the saddle had made me greedy and keen, but I controlled myself and entered her slowly, an inch at a time, before giving her the lot in a final stroke. She moaned and rubbed herself against me, grinding against the stairs and my groin. She came before I did, and I decided to be a gentleman.

'Why don't we finish this off somewhere more comfortable?' I suggested.

She nodded, eyes half closed, and we collected ourselves and headed up to her flat. There I was rewarded for my efforts: under the polite, nervous exterior was a girl who'd clearly spent a lot of her time as a recent singleton reading sex manuals or learning from experts. She had an amazing appetite for all things male. She found three or four ways in which to come that I'd only read about. For one orgasm, she had me lie back with my legs up, before she sat on my cock. The pressure made it taught against her inside, and she wriggled down so it was deep against her, stroking her G-spot against its head until she was screaming with pleasure.

After that, her small hands could not stay away from me. She bent over and let me fuck her from behind, but stopped me from coming with a swift tweak of the balls. She moved off me, then sucked me until I came in her mouth. For the next time, she rode me until she came, leaning back on my thighs while she pulled her own nipples hard. Then she sucked me off again and made me come on her tits, lick it up, and kiss it into her mouth.

Once we'd exhausted each other, she skipped away from the bed and put on a dressing gown.

'I don't want you to stay, I hope that's OK?'

Surprised, I looked at her.

'No?'

'No. I've had fun. I may call you.'

'You may call me?'

'Yeah. You know. If I want another fuck. Yeah?'

For the first time in my life, I felt dirty, and I felt used.

It was a wonderful feeling.

Chapter Fifteen

While the work situation didn't improve, my state of mind certainly did.

I soon realised that understatement was the way of the Web: anyone seeking a 'long-term' relationship had a set of shackles already at hand. But at the other end, 'fun' or 'no strings' was very often a free pass to a world of sexual enthusiasm.

It wasn't so much that people lied. I mean, some people did, from men alluding to improbable measurements to women skirting round the fact that they were trying to get impregnated, by anyone, now. It was more a matter of knowing your public.

I signed up with a couple of different sites; each seemed to have slightly different requirements, and slightly different clientele. One sight was photo heavy, so I loaded up an old pic from when I was trying to make a go of it as an actor. I was quite pleased with the effect, and the years hadn't been so hard that I could be accused of fraud.

Another site was more about chat and charm, so I cobbled together my best personal profile and sat back and waited. Again, I played up the self-deprecating humour and borrowed a couple of stories that friends had told.

Another site was more interactive, with people coming and going online, chats starting up and dates being arranged. Given my employment situation, I had time on my hands and no boss looking over my shoulder and forcing me into a speedy alt+tab manoeuvre.

Sitting in the pub with my laptop, waiting for either

the jobcentre or one agency or another not to ring, I fashioned myself for my different audiences. And the results were impressive.

My professional photo on the website with lots of pictures seemed to have a particular strength: it got me dates with very posh girls. One girl was the daughter of some earl, duke or other nob. My father would probably know the title. I've never been very big on aristos. She emailed me asking if I fancied supper (her words, not mine). I agreed, and she said she'd pick me up at seven. I liked the fact that she had a car, but didn't like the fact that she wouldn't be drinking – it always relaxes things a little, you know.

But I'd misread her email: what she had said was that she would have me picked up at seven, and have me picked up she did, as a car almost too big to fit up our street appeared and I got a text to wait downstairs. The girl was nowhere to be seen, and I was guided into the spacious interior of a Rolls by a butler who'd been resurrected just long enough for the assignment, and resentfully grumbled his way through delivering a shag to his employer's little girl.

It was a good gig, I'll admit. She was some society heiress who'd been ditched by her fiancé, and although the very attractive picture she'd posted was more or less true, she'd been using her middle name and some distant aunt's surname as cover. I was sworn to secrecy before I'd got so much as through the door of her suite at a rather exclusive Mayfair private members club.

The setting was great, the set-up fantastic; the sex, I must say, was disappointing: a lot of barked orders and, when she did eventually come, the disconcerting experience of hearing a girl in her early twenties cry out 'daddy'. It almost put me off my stroke.

She seemed to get pissed off at my presence almost as soon as we separated. I ran a finger down her spine, hoping to let her know that there was plenty more if she wanted it, but she stalked away from the bed, disappeared into an anteroom or possibly just the toilet and returned almost totally hidden by a thick dressing gown.

After a few minutes of surprisingly awkward silence – bearing in mind quite how vocal she'd been when ordering me to smack her arse cheeks as I fucked her from behind – I got the message and pulled on some clothes, and then left with little more ado. I even turned down the offer of another chauffeur ride home.

Thinking about it, I think she was surprised at how much she'd been able to let go. I imagine her ex was some chinless inbred who could only get it up while looking at a portrait of his stately home and horses, whereas centuries of breeding on her side had designed a woman meant to close her eyes, lie back, open her legs and think of England, rather than the cross between a camp commandant and a vixen on heat that she'd shown herself capable of being. As I'd been there to see the performance, she wanted rid of me as soon as possible. I never saw her again, except in the papers a few weeks later, when her engagement to a Byelorussian billionaire was announced.

Chapter Sixteen

Being shagged and dumped has never been too much of a problem for me, and I got over the business with the heiress in, well, seconds, I guess.

Within a couple of days, I still had no job, but did have a couple more dates, this time from the profile I had online. I'd met a couple of girls via chat room websites. One thing they all seemed to have in common was that their constant need to exchange gossip, titbits and rumours was not just limited to the Web.

One of the women I met was married, in her forties and keen on fancy jewellery and frilly knickers. Her husband worked on oil rigs, and so she had money to spare and six months of the year to herself, one on, one off, when her husband was away. I got the impression that as well as having a high sex drive that needed satisfying, for six months she also needed some company, but from someone who wasn't going to make demands on the rest of her life.

We met quite regularly for three weeks or so. Her husband had gone away and, as ever, she was back online with a false name, looking for fun. We met after exchanging a series of flirty emails and messages, and after a couple of drinks, found ourselves back at her place. She lived further out of the city, up the hill, in an area full of fancy old apartment blocks and expensive Sixties maisonettes. She and her absent husband lived halfway up an elegant building with excellent views of the park and a lift that took you straight into their hall. The flat was lit with uplighters and spotlights, and around the walls were memorabilia from their travels, generally to countries with large fossil fuel reserves.

She was a woman who worked hard to look after herself. I don't think she'd ever been pretty, but she was striking, and her outfit – a leather skirt and tight blouse – was sexy and suited her.

From the first time we went to bed though, I realised that there was something strange about the sex. Although she was an experienced and very pleasurable lover, with a technique that made up for any lack of purely physical attractiveness, I got the impression that part of the reason she was so willing to fuck in almost any position imaginable, as well as enjoying using vibrators, whips and other toys, was that it was a preamble to something else.

An example: somehow, we ended up talking about group sex. She said she'd never been with more than one man at once, but would like to, or at least know what it felt like. After we'd been screwing for a few minutes, she produced the vibrator that I'd used to warm her up. Her pussy was very wet, and I found a tube of lube. I pulled out of her and gently moistened her with the gel. Then I entered her, and once I was half inside, I slowly introduced the vibrator. She gasped as it slid in, tight against my own cock, and then moaned with pleasure once I'd turned it on. We both came, noisily and enthusiastically, only a couple of minutes later.

But these sorts of games and experiments just seemed to pass by. Really, what she seemed to want was the time afterward, the pillow talk, as we lay amongst discarded dildos and torn tie-up knickers, and she told me one element or another of her life story or someone else's. The sex was great, which was great for me, but that wasn't really what she was interested in me for. I was something like a store for spare words.

I didn't mind – particularly as she was willing to indulge and indeed encourage pretty much any sort of pleasure that came to mind. But it was obvious when, a few weeks later with her husband back from offshore, she stopped calling, that I or whoever else was just serving time.

Chapter Seventeen

We're taking a roundabout route to get there, I realise, but the story of how I became a call guy isn't simple.

People often ask about the first time, and I guess the first time I took cash for sex was sort of because of my Internet dates. That's why I say it's all Celeste's fault. Before that moment I'd thought that I was getting something for nothing. I'd had a pretty good few weeks, with a few different girls, and although I was still no closer to anything like employment, I was feeling a lot better about things.

It's a big gap between having lots of enjoyable casual sex to fucking for money or sex becoming a way of earning a living. There are a lot of people who don't have the good fortune to enjoy the former before the latter. For those who do take the step, it's a major change.

I guess that what changed was realising that I didn't need to feel grateful for getting sex. Even more, I discovered that quite a few women had thought that they were getting something for nothing from me. There were even some, in fact quite a few of them, who were willing to make it worth my while.

After a few weeks of fairly regular success via Internet dating, I was in a good position to keep to my standards. That's not to say all my dates had ended in riotous screwing. A couple had been perfectly pleasant and polite but gone nowhere. On a few occasions, it took dates, plural, to get into the sack. And there'd been a couple of girls who I'd just not gotten on with. One gave the strong impression from after about three minutes that she thought I was a prick and wanted to be somewhere else as soon as possible.

So far, you might have got the impression that I'm pretty indiscriminate in the matter of who I share a bed with. But I do have standards, and there are types of women I prefer to others. Obviously in a professional capacity, I keep this to myself. But in the days when it was just for pleasure, I was, well, if not exactly choosy, certainly not likely to go with just anyone. I may not have mentioned it before, but in some of the cases where a date went nowhere, I was as glad as the girl.

It wasn't just a looks thing; sure, there were some I didn't fancy. But unless you can persuade her to do something particularly perverse, there's only so much fun to be had shagging with a girl who you find annoying, who thinks you're a moron or whose voice sets your teeth on edge.

But it wasn't quite like that with my first Jenny. Let's call her J. for short.

J. was quite a few years older than me, smartly dressed, perhaps with slightly too much make-up, but not so much as to make me look for the tidemark. Our date was in a wine bar, at the bottom of Regent Street. It was a funny venue, underground, full of businessmen in double-breasted suits and in the company of their secretaries and PAs. It was as if the world of work and socialising had stopped in about 1978.

I was probably the youngest person there by about ten years, and although we got on fine, never at any stage did I feel that there was a spark between us. I'll be blunt – for the first time in a while, I was out with a date and wasn't imagining what she'd be like naked or, better still, expensively almost naked and posed compromisingly on a bed.

Somehow or another, probably to do with me not paying attention to proceedings properly, or misreading the signs, we ended up back at her place. We continued a fairly pointless conversation about congestion charging and smoking in public, made doubly pointless by the fact that I don't have a car and don't smoke. I'm going to sound like a bush-tease, or whatever the male equivalent is, but I realised at one moment, close to midnight, that I was going to have to come up with some sort of excuse to leave. After she offered me another coffee, or the option of going somewhere more comfortable, I checked my watch and half faked a yawn.

'I'd love to. But I've got a really busy day tomorrow.'

'Really.'

'Yeah, yeah, I mean I probably should be, you know, getting along.'

'Right.'

'Work, you know.'

'Cesc, is that normally how you end these dates?'

I hesitated. 'Well, sometimes. I guess it depends.' I immediately realised how bad the line sounded.

'On what?' she asked coldly.

'Look, I don't want to have a row. I think I should just go.'

'Don't worry. I know the answer. It depends on whether you fancy her or not.'

I couldn't think of anything like a sensible comeback.

'Yes. Look, I'll be honest. I guess you're just not my type.'

She looked at me for a few seconds.

'Well at least you're honest. What is your type?'

'I don't really have a set one. Shit. You know what I mean.'

She seemed to think for a few moments.

66

'OK. That's fine. But let's be frank. You're a barman right?'

'Yeah. Well, was. In fact, I was fired. I was also an actor, briefly.'

'So I'll be honest, as you've been good enough to be honest with me. I really want a fuck, and I guess you must need the money. So I'll pay you. We both get what we want.'

'Isn't that illegal?'

She shrugged. 'We can have sex. I'll give you some money. It's not like you're working the street.'

'I guess so,' I said, starting to feel persuaded.

'I can tell you need the money. Haven't you seen me before?'

'No.' I racked my memory. 'Oh … maybe …'

'That's right. I've seen you at the jobcentre. I'm a consultant for your caseworker's boss. Well, his boss's boss, really.'

'Well should you be encouraging me to fuck for money? Surely that would be a breach of my jobseeker's allowance?'

'I think we could probably turn a blind eye this once.'

I hesitated.

'Is this bribery or blackmail?'

'Neither. Both,' she said, with a faint smile.

I thought for a moment.

'How much?' I asked.

'£100.'

'£150,' I said quickly.

She paused and looked at me, I guess calculating my worth.

'OK,' she said. 'But I hope you're good.'

And the funny thing was, despite not particularly fancying her, despite the very unromantic build-up, I was, and so was she. It was something about getting paid for it that made my very conscious of doing things a certain way. If there is such a thing as a correct way, then I made sure to do it the correct way. And it must have been something to do with the fact that she was paying that she seemed absolutely determined to enjoy it.

'Tell me what you want,' I said to her, as we stood and headed towards the bedroom.

'Oh, I think you'll work it out.'

The first thing I worked out is that there's never a huge amount of kissing in professional sex. Mouth to mouth, that is, as we both spent a lot of time kissing other parts. What there is of it is, at most, preliminary and polite. As we sat down on her bed, I shifted to her neck, running my hands up through her hair as I slipped her top and the strap of her bra off her shoulder. I shifted round to sit behind her, and massaged her shoulders, her back, and then round to her breasts. Her large breasts were soon out of their bra, and I worked smooth circles around them before tousling her nipples into hard points.

I pulled off her top and threw off my own and lay her down on her front, running my hands along her spine, massaging her shoulders and pressing my erection between her legs through our clothes. Her breathing was getting deeper and huskier, and I pressed our bodies together as I reached down, running my hands up her front and cupping her breasts.

Then I unzipped her skirt to reveal a tiny thong. It didn't quite suit her figure, but hey, I'm a professional. I rubbed her calves, her thighs, and then worked my palms around her buttocks and up the inside of her thighs. I could tell from the way she was arching her back and lifting her hips that her pussy was calling out for me.

Still on top of her, I reached around her hips and slid my hands into her knickers. She was totally shaved, and already soaking wet.

I rolled her over and began to lick and tease her nipples, while my fingers tickled over her clit and lips. She arched her back and spread her legs, inviting me. I kissed my way down her body, probing her belly button with my tongue, before kissing and running the tip of my tongue over her mound of Venus and inner thighs. I ran my tongue along her clit and then used it to separate her lips. Soon I had her clit in my mouth, licking and sucking it between my lips. Each time she seemed close to coming, her moans and gasps getting louder, I pulled away, ran my hands up to cup her tits, and then entered her with my tongue.

'I'm not going to let you come quite yet,' I said, leaning back away from her. I stripped from the waist and then slid a condom on. As she lay there, eyes half closed, legs wide, pussy wet with my saliva and her juices, I saw her hand creeping down her body towards her sex.

'Now don't start thinking about finishing yourself off yet,' I said. 'There's plenty of time for that.' I grabbed her hand, pushed it away, and with the other hand, turned her over onto her front. I pressed myself down onto her and entered her from behind, our bodies both flat, mine pressing her down onto the bed. I fucked her slowly at first, long deep strokes from behind, while she grasped my hands and I kept her pinned to the bed. I could feel from her movement and breathing that she was close to coming.

'Not yet,' I said, pulling out. She gasped with the sudden emptiness inside her.

My cock still rock hard, I rolled her back over and

returned to licking her clit. She was quivering all over, and as she neared her climax, her moans and cries turned into squeals and shrieks.

'Now, now, yes. I want you to come inside me, now!' she managed to shout.

As I pulled away, she sat up, pushing me backwards and quickly mounting me. She rode me hard, while I strummed her clit with one hand and teased a nipple with the other. She began to call out, her motion getting more and more rapid and frantic with each thrust, and soon we were both coming in arching, bouncing movements, her pussy dripping wet onto my crotch.

After the first effort, as we lay, separated and panting, on the bed, she looked up at me.

'Are we costing by time or by orgasm?' she asked.

'No idea. Isn't it a flat rate?' I replied.

'In that case …' she said.

'What?' I replied.

'Come here.'

I moved towards her, and she was soon sucking my cock back hard again. The second session was even more energetic, as I fucked her hard from behind, flat against the bed, to another noisy orgasm.

Exhausted, I left in the early hours of the morning, £150 pounds richer and, officially, a paid shag.

Chapter Eighteen

I was sitting outside a pub by the canal in Camden with Celeste a few days later when I got the call. She'd been taking the piss out of me because of my tired eyes and irregular early morning arrivals. I told her that since she'd been seeing her new man she'd been walking like a cowboy, and she told me to piss off.

A couple of American tourists sharing the table next to us were giving Cel dirty looks as her tobacco smoke floated past their lunches and towards the Lock, when my phone rang. I didn't recognise the number: another mobile, no clues.

'Another date?' she asked.

'Jealous?' I said.

'No. You dick.'

I pulled a face and answered.

'Chesc,' the female voice on the other end mispronounced.

'Yeah,' I said, trying not to correct her.

'I hear you fuck for money.'

I almost dropped my phone.

'Can I call you back?' I asked.

'Yeah. Just don't take too long about it.'

I hung up.

'Shit,' I said to Celeste. The couple gave me a dirty look.

'What?'

'Erm. It's rather a delicate matter,' I said. The couple next to us shifted awkwardly. I looked around for another table. They were all taken on what was a rare warm and rain-free day.

'Celeste,' I whispered, trying hard not to be heard. 'Did I tell you about the consultant woman?' She raised her eyes to the heavens.

'I told you. You have an addiction.' She turned to the couple. 'This is my friend Cesc, by the way. He's got a sex addiction. In fact, he's got *the* sex addiction. He's going to be in the medical textbooks.'

'Look, fuck off, Cel. This is serious. I need your advice.' Turning to the couple, I added, 'And I'm sorry about her. She has a serious case of vibrator-stuck-in-arse syndrome. It affects her motor and vocal functions. It's like Tourette's, but twelve inches and pink.'

Muttering and fussing, the couple stood up and left, the man throwing a twenty onto the table and leaving his sandwich half finished.

'I'm sorry,' I said. 'I don't mean to offend.' They ignored me and left.

'Seriously, Cel. I think I may have accidentally become a male prostitute.'

'I didn't know you liked cock,' she answered.

'No, you idiot. With women.'

She sat back and took a sip on her outsized cocktail.

'Really. Who'd pay you?'

'Seemingly at least two women,' I said.

She nodded her head.

'Who? And, more importantly, how?'

I related briefly the incident with my caseworker's boss's boss's consultant. Or boss's boss's boss, whatever it was.

'That sounds more like blackmail than prostitution. I'm surprised she didn't threaten you with jail. What's she look like?'

'She's not hideous.'

'You really know how to flatter a girl,' Celeste said

72

with a shake of the head.

'Well, she's OK. But not really my type. She's a few years older than us.'

'You don't know my age, kiddo.'

'Does it matter as you act your cup size?'

'That doesn't make sense. How can you act a letter?'

'Look, this is getting off the point. Basically, I took the money, no questions asked, gave her an absolutely fantastic screw, and now it sounds like her pals want a piece of the Cesc.'

'The Cesc? That's so 1950s, you knob. Do you have a quiff and a leather jacket?'

'I guess if the assignment requires it. Cel, you know enough about sleeping with people for money. How does it work?'

I got the sentence out just before the slap connected.

'Do you want my help or not?' she said, while I straightened my jaw. Meanwhile, the sun had gone in, and I realised that people were looking at us.

'Can you manage not to smoke for a few minutes? Can we go inside?'

We moved indoors into a space that despite the lack of smokers had a floor the colour of a diseased lung and a strong smell of detergent. I could see that Celeste was trying to find a way to walk and sit that involved touching as little as possible. I even got the impression that she was avoiding breathing excessively.

I bought another round of drinks.

'Feeling flush, eh?' said Celeste as I returned.

'Yeah. Maybe. Anyway, what do you think I should do?'

'Well, I mean, you accepted the money once. Why not again?'

'She caught me in a moment of weakness.'

73

'Right. She caught you with a hole in your wallet and a boner in your pants, more like.'

'Celeste, I never realised you were a poet.'

'Seriously though,' she continued, sipping a G&T through a straw that barely touched her lips. 'We all do some cruddy things for money. Or in your case, do absolutely nothing for very little money. I don't see any reason not to.'

'Isn't it illegal?'

'So's anal sex, but so what?'

'Is it?'

'I think so.'

'Why aren't you in jail then?'

'Cesc, actually do fuck off.'

I raised my hands in apology.

'Sorry. But look, isn't this just the slightest bit dodgy?'

'Dodgier than cruising contact websites for casual sex with strangers?'

'Is that dodgy?'

'Do you tell anyone?'

'You.'

'You don't need to tell me. I can hear you.'

I took a swig of my drink.

'OK. Point taken. So you're not taking the piss. If you were me, you'd return the call and go with this girl.'

'Well I'm not a lesbian. And if it was a bloke calling, then no, not with a barge pole. But if I were you, then yes. It's different for girls.'

'How so?'

'You'd be more of a novelty.'

'That's the nicest thing you've ever said to me,' I said.

'And, you're less likely to be kidnapped and chopped

74

up into little pieces by some deranged loner. I mean, maybe I'd go, but I'd take a big friend and a Tazer.'

'That'd put him right in the mood, I'm sure.'

Celeste fiddled with her shades for a moment.

'It's tricky,' she said. 'I think people are still sexist. I certainly wouldn't want it to get out if I were taking money for sex.'

'But you are …' I interrupted.

'Do you want another slap? I can't help it if men can be very generous with me. But at least I know them in the first place. Not some stranger who's got my number at the jobcentre.'

'You wouldn't know what a jobcentre is. But I take the point. I'd actually quite like it if people suggested that it was worth paying money to have sex with me. So you think I should call her back?'

She paused, sniffed her drink, and took out a cigarette while looking at the door.

'Now I wasn't saying that. Not exactly. But I don't think you shouldn't.'

I added up the negatives. It was about as close to a straight answer as I was going to get from my friend.

Chapter Nineteen

Another drink went by, Celeste popped outside for a couple more cigarettes and I sat looking at the mystery number.

I didn't call immediately, and I sort of half chickened out of making a decision. Back at the flat, Celeste prepared for an evening with some college friends of hers, most of who had married extremely wealthy young men and were now busying themselves in the pursuit of perfection as modern wives. I sat on the sofa, playing with my phone and failing to watch TV.

After much delaying, I finally sent the mystery woman a text. It said, simply, 'You can call me now.'

She was clearly waiting. My phone rang right back.

'Where were we?' she asked.

'Erm. Fucking for money?' I answered.

'Yes. Well?'

'Well what?'

'Do you?'

'That depends.' I realised that despite spending so long thinking and talking about it, it hadn't really gone to plan. More to the point, I didn't have a plan.

'On what?'

I realised that there was a strong chance of things going very quickly wrong.

'Whether we can count on our mutual discretion in a professional relationship.' As the words left my mouth, I wondered who on earth had said them for me.

'I say,' mocked the woman on the other end. I tried to imagine her physically from the voice. She sounded older than me, like a smoker, and had a touch of wickedness about her.

She continued. 'So, do you want to do this then?'

'Yes. I need some details. And we need to agree terms.'

'I'll text you my address. What do you normally charge?'

I invented a figure that sounded reasonable.

'And what does that get me?'

'Anything you want, unless it involves long-term harm to me or a third party. And I don't go with other men, children or animals.'

'Of course. You're a gentleman, after all.'

I hadn't been called that for a while, but I agreed all the same.

'And is that a night, an evening or what?'

'Until you want rid of me.'

'Wow. And what if I wear you out?'

'We'll see, shall we,' I answered.

'OK then. I'm looking forward to it.'

'Good. I'll see you later then,' I said, and hung up.

I still wasn't convinced. I thought she might not text, and after a few minutes, when the message still hadn't arrived, I thought it might have been a wind-up. But the text arrived, and I thought it might still be a wind-up, and that I should either sack it off or take a friend, preferably one who was good at fighting and/or legal advice.

I looked up the address online: it was a swanky new apartment block not far from the flat. I checked the property developer's website: private gym, swimming pool, views over the heath. Perhaps I should have asked for more money. I figured that at least if things got ugly, there'd be a concierge to rescue me. I realised that I'd have to get a taxi if I wanted to turn up looking pristine, and wondered if I should add that or include it in the price. I also thought hard about whether I should add VAT.

In the end, I concluded that if the worst came to the worst, I could just leg it and put the whole thing down to experience. If she'd got my details from J., then it would probably count in my favour if I had to report her for harassing me. Offering someone money for sex is one thing, I reckoned; passing them on to someone else is at least a step further.

So, I showered and shaved, slung on some CKs, some fancy clothes and a dash of aftershave and made a quick check on my condom supply. As I waited for the taxi, I could feel the adrenalin and the testosterone starting to flow. Even if she wasn't a great looker, I was enthusiastic about getting another performance like the other night.

The taxi was early, so I took him a roundabout route to get a better look at the area and the building. I don't know why. I knew that part of London well, but I suppose I was looking for any sort of sign. I'm not superstitious, but I guessed that if the flat was surrounded by police cars, I might give it a miss.

There was nothing untoward, and nothing to give me an excuse to duck out of it. As the taxi pulled up, I caught a glimpse of someone looking down, three or four storeys up, on the other side of some gates and an elegantly paved and gravelled entrance way.

I buzzed and the big glass door opened on to a wide marble hallway without a word from the intercom. She was obviously waiting for me. The lift sped me to her floor, and as I stepped out, I realised, all of a sudden, quite how much I was looking forward to it.

Chapter Twenty

One thing that's important about this game is the erection.

If it can't perform to order, or a guy can't find a way to cheat nature, then he shouldn't even try. Or he needs to grow one hell of a tongue.

Now the erection is a curious thing: if any other part of the body increased so greatly in size and stood out at that sort of angle, you'd see a doctor. When you get one in the wrong context, you seldom mention it, unless you're a radio shock DJ or one of those American sports commentators who get far too excited about athletic endeavour.

In this profession, I've discovered that timing is all-important. If you walk into a job with the fellow already stiff as a board and bulging in your pants, you may give the impression that you're just totally indiscriminate. On top of that, there's no contrast.

The trick is to let the client know that she makes it hard. I'm not saying I douse it in ice before turning up, but it's good to make it clear that the performance is being laid on especially. Prior to dates, I may drift off into fantasy or memories of previous sessions, just to put me in the right frame of mind. But nowadays I always make sure that it comes up for her and just for her.

That evening, however, even before I'd met her, I was walking gingerly, my cock throbbing with expectation. I was surprised at myself; I suspected at least some nerves, but the whole experience surrounding the assignment was very exciting.

When the lift pinged to a halt, the doors opened on to

a carpeted hall. Along the corridor, tastefully and discreetly decorated with some prints and a vase of flowers on a sideboard, was an open door. I padded over and then knocked.

'If you're the delivery man, come in.'

I considered any one of a number of puns I'd heard in soft porn, and rejected them all. Instead, I pushed the door open.

'I'm afraid not,' I said to no one in particular. 'It's Cesc. We spoke on the phone, earlier.'

Inside, I surveyed the room. It was a wide, open-plan kitchen, diner, living room in one, with distinct sections and modern furniture over a dark wooden floor. Very elegant. The far wall was floor-to-ceiling glass, giving a magnificent view of the city.

'Anyone home?' I called.

There was no response. I shut the door behind me and looked for signs of life or habitation. To my right was a kitchen area, next to it, closer to the window, was a long dining table. The left of the room held sofas, a TV, a couple of very large art prints of discreet female nudes, and a large sheepskin rug. In either corner, left and right, doors led off to, I presume, bedrooms.

I clicked over to the window. I noticed a couple more interesting features: a large coffee table book of what appeared to be contemporary erotic photographs. And in the glass cabinet by the sofas, quite a number of books on sex. I started to draw a mental picture of the woman's interests. It did nothing to quell my arousal.

'Hello,' I said again. Again, there was no response.

On the table was a tray, with a glass, some ice and white wine. I poured myself a drink and stood surveying the scene and the view. I noticed that one of the doors was open, and the other was closed. I tried to work out whether this was clue or coincidence. I walked back across the room. By the entrance, there were no hints: no little notes, no lipstick messages. On the floor, there were no trails of underwear. I called out again, but again with no reply.

I deliberated for a while. It was clearly some sort of game. As I understood it, I was paid to play by the client's rules.

'I have a delivery for you,' I said, quietly, but loud enough to be heard in either room. A voice from directly behind me made me jump.

'Pick a door,' it said.

One was closed, the other half open.

I chose the closed door. Half-open doors have always made me suspicious.

I tried the handle, but it was locked. I noticed that there was a fisheye. I knocked, and stood back from the door slightly. After a moment, I heard the bolt being turned.

I tried again. This time the door opened.

The room was darkly lit: the light through the drapes as the sun began to set, a vintage lamp in the corner and some candles. The decor was dark, mostly: long black velvet curtains, black and white prints on the walls, a line of black lacquer-fronted cupboards, a full-length mirror on a stand in the corner. And a very big bed, made up in what, in the faint light, looked like black satin.

There was no one. While the room suggested gothic perversions, the absence of another person suggested a wasted trip. I half checked that there was no one hiding in a corner. I was right. There was no one hiding in the corner. I muttered something to myself and went to turn, only to be intercepted by two hands over my eyes.

'Don't move,' said a sensual female voice.

'Not moving,' I said. 'Only my lips.'

I could tell she was at least my height, although a sharp click of metal on hardwood suggested that she was wearing stilettos.

'What are you delivering?' she asked, close to my ear. I felt the hairs on the back of my neck stand up.

'Whatever you want,' I replied.

'Good.'

Very slowly, I moved my hands behind me. I felt what I thought were hips, and was pleased to feel smooth flesh and silk. With a very small movement, I pulled her close to me. Her hands went from my eyes to my lips to my chest. Against my back I could feel her nipples through the fabric of her clothes.

'Can I turn round now?' I asked.

'Not yet.'

With her hands still over my eyes, we walked forward towards the bed, stopping just short.

'I've left the money for you in an envelope on the dining table. I'm presuming you know what you're doing.'

'That's correct,' I said, passing over the fact that despite my amateur experience I was still very much a novice professional.

'Good. What do you think I want?'

I considered the surroundings, the heavy scent in the air and the heat from the candles.

'I try not to make predictions. But I think one of us is going to get bound and gagged.'

'Correct,' she said.

As I opened my mouth to attempt a witty response, her knees knocked into the back of mine, throwing me off balance. Her hands went to my shoulders as I fell and

82

I was spun round onto my back on the bed. I noticed a large iron bedstead as I landed, and then caught a glimpse of her: at least a decade older than me, with raven hair cut sternly around her face and very pale skin over dramatic, aquiline features. She was tall and slim, but with large breasts in a push-up bra. Over her underwear – a thong and stockings, I judged from the outline – was a long, black silk dress, slit right up to the hip on both sides. She was not pretty, but she was magnificent.

As she pounced on me, there was a metallic sound: before I could react, cuffs were on my wrists and I was strapped to the frame.

'If at any stage you want to stop, say so, and we stop,' she said.

'Let's hope that's not necessary,' I replied, testing my bonds.

'Right. Well in that case, just knock the board three times.'

'Why?' I asked, before she answered my question by forcing a bit between my teeth and a strap around the back of my head: a gag. I'd been right.

Despite the physical discomfort, I was excited by the scene. She looked down on me from by the bed, and then very slowly undid my shirt and trousers. My erection was fighting to get out, and soon she had stripped me, leaving me naked bar an undone shirt. Then she was at the foot of the bed, and I felt a larger version of the wrist cuffs on my ankles. Soon I was fully stretched on the bed, my erection like a sundial on its stand.

'In our everyday lives,' she said, 'we too often ignore those senses that are not vision or taste. Everything is eaten or looked at these days. Sensations become dulled. And people are selfish. No one takes pleasure in giving sensations to others.'

I started a response: 'Normally that's my job.' It came out as 'Orhhuhhy ah aehh ohh.'

'Precisely,' she said.

She moved towards me and produced from the same hidden pocket that had housed the cuffs, a long, black silk handkerchief. She tied it over my eyes and firmly knotted it behind my head. I thought about struggling against the bonds, as part of the game, but decided to keep still.

The next thing I knew was the feeling of hands on me: slim, slightly cold fingers running over my chest, across my stomach, around my crotch, down my thighs, and back up again. They ran in circles over my chest and then were gone. I tried to work out where she was, but I could only assume that she was standing astride me. The hands returned and I felt them on my nipples, first massaging, then teasing, then tweaking. And then there was a cold, metallic sensation, then pressure, and the pain.

I bit against the gag, trying to identify the precise source of the pain. I was sure metal clamps had been applied. This was clearly a woman who had invested in the correct equipment.

After a moment in which I began to adjust to the new sensation, I felt her hands again. Now they were massaging my thighs, my abdomen, my groin. Then I felt a tickle against my balls, and the lightest of touches along the length of my dick. I arched my back, straining for more contact, and then she was gone.

A few seconds later, there was a change: instead of her hands, I felt something like a feather being run over my body, alternating tickling and arousal. Its tip moved over my balls, up my cock, over its head. And then she was gone again.

The next sensation was metallic, cold against my thighs. And then I heard her voice.

'This will most likely hurt,' she said. I felt her hands running up and down my shaft, and then one of them cupping my balls. Soon the cup became a squeeze, and the cold metal applied itself either side of the top of my sac. I felt it tighten, and then felt it pull down. The pain was intense, but my cock hardened. I squirmed, trying to find some way of losing the vice that was pulling on my testicles, or somewhere to stick my penis. There was nothing.

'Don't think I just want you for your cock, Cesc,' she said. I realised she had moved, and was further away.

'Although I might do,' she said, from closer. And then I felt her mouth around me: there was no other contact, just suddenly the hot flesh of her lips and tongue around my penis. I felt myself starting to come, but strained every muscle to stop. My balls tried to rise against the clamp but a second later she was off me and the clamp was pulled and tightened. I tried to wince with pain.

'Not so fast,' she said. I heard her walk away and heard the clink of ice in a glass. Then I felt the shock of the cold water poured over my cock and balls. I felt them tense, but not shrink. Numbness came over my groin, and meanwhile she took my cock roughly in her hand.

Now she was wearing gloves. At first, I thought they were silk, but in between the delicious smoothness, there was something else: a painful abrasiveness that hurt and aroused at once. More specially made kit, I thought, trying to control a mixture of feelings including the need to cry out in pain and the urgent need to come.

Just before reaching the point of being unbearable,

everything stopped. There was a pause, and then she undid the nipple clamps. I sighed with relief, only to be immediately more aware of the pain in my penis and testicles. After a second, I felt a liquid sensation: she ran ice over my chest and massaged it over my nipples. The chill was then replaced with intense cold, before I realised it was heat, burning heat: I felt singeing pain and then dull tension, and bit hard against the gag: she was pouring hot wax onto me, first onto my nipples, then onto my stomach and finally onto my balls.

My heart was now pounding. I thought about knocking the headboard, but resisted. Pain, I thought, was just one sensation amongst many, and unless I heard the buzz of a chainsaw, I hoped I was more or less safe. I simply had to bite the bullet, as it were, and try to enjoy myself. Certainly, none of her actions had lessened my arousal.

With the wax hardened on me, I felt her over me again. Hoping that the binding and singeing had been a prelude to a fuck, I expected to feel her close to me. But I soon realised that she was concentrating on something else: quickly, my right hand was unhooked, crossed with the left and refastened. At the bottom of the bed, the same happened to my feet. With a push, she left me lying face down. 'Oh shit,' I thought.

I felt the first crack of the whip, or crop, or birch, hard against my buttocks. The pain was still registering as she hit my thighs, my buttocks again and then my calves. She was clever: the strap was thick enough to hurt, intensely, but did not seem to cut. I felt my breath quicken and I bit on the gag tight, before another volley of shots numbed my legs and arse.

I realised also that I was lying face down, and the sensation of the sheets against my cock was going to make me come at some stage if I wasn't careful. Clearly, so did she. I felt a sharp pain in my balls and realised that the screw had been pulled up. Now I was on all fours, my balls pulling away from my body, my cock tantalisingly in mid air. She beat my arse, my legs and, in a blow that caused me almost to gag and to howl with pain, my poor, exposed balls.

And then there was nothing. I had a chance to feel the various echoes of mistreatment over my body. I breathed hard through my nose, and tried to become as comfortable as possible.

'Well done, Mr Aleixandre,' she said. I realised that the voice was behind me. 'You've taken a lot so far.'

I pondered the implications of 'so far'.

'I don't want to ruin you the first time,' she said, now from beneath me. I felt her hands on my cock, and suddenly, there was a condom on me. I strained to move downwards, but felt the pain as my balls were pulled back against their strap.

'Now, I want you to fuck me. As hard as you like,' she said. I could only move so far down without splitting my reproductive organs in two, but somehow, I felt her rise to meet me. Her underwear was gone, although the long silk dress and her stockings appeared to be on still. I tried to thrust, but each push brought intense pain with the resistance against my testicles. She'd obviously been turned on by the act, as she moaned with pleasure with no more than half of me inside her. I tried to thrust, but could not, but she squirmed and arched beneath me, drawing me into her. Again, I pushed, and the pain grew. We were moving together, I with my limbs still stretched, she running her hands all over me, occasionally allowing her nipples to brush against me.

Suddenly, I felt a release: she had unhooked the leash,

or it had come unhooked, more likely, as she seemed surprised. My weight fell forward onto her, and my cock pushed deep inside her. I felt a rush that was almost the prelude to coming, but I lifted back my head and held on. I fucked hard, almost angrily, clearly to her taste. I could feel her rubbing her clit against me, savouring the sensation, and soon she was coming with noisy screams, many of which included strange abuse, swear words and desperate pleas for more, harder. Soon she was shaking beneath me, but I was not finished. I controlled myself and then doubled my efforts, rubbing hard against her while thrusting quickly and insistently deep inside her. She came again, biting hard into my neck.

As she shook underneath me, something strange happened: I felt the bonds on my wrists come loose. I lost my balance and found myself half falling off her. Without coming, I pulled out of her and then, before she had quite realised what was happening, I spun her round beneath me. I pushed my knees between her legs and grasped her wrist with one hand, and pressed her down, from behind. With the other hand, I separated her lips and guided my cock into her.

Once I was in, I held both her wrists firmly against the bed. My weight on her, I slid deeper inside. She gasped, part in pleasure, part in surprise, and did again as, having grasped both wrists with one hand, I slid a finger between her buttocks, and then further in. Then I released her hands, and with my free hand, I spanked her buttocks, gently at first, then harder. Soon, she came again, calling me a series of filthy names, her sex pulsating around me. I pushed my finger deeper inside her, and then with the harshest of spanks so far gave a final thrust and felt myself ejaculate, hard and for a long time, my balls rising against the clamp.

Once I'd come, I pulled off the blindfold and managed to undo my wrists and balls. She was lying, face down, a catlike grin about her face. I loosened the ankle straps and found some clothes. There was a bathroom en suite, where I picked off the wax and examined myself for any obvious signs of injury. I'd got away more or less unscathed.

Back out in the room, she was sitting back up, her hair wildly ruffled and her dress askew.

'Cesc, erm, I hope you don't think …'

I cut her off with a gesture.

'Same time next week?' I said.

A smirk crossed her face. She nodded. I took the money on the table and left.

Chapter Twenty-one

I was sitting in a café in Primrose Hill with Celeste when she noticed the scars: a deep bite mark on my neck and a singe on my face where I suppose that some wax must have gone astray.

'Whatever have you been getting up to?' she asked.

'I saw that woman.'

'Which one?'

'The one who texted me. The one who got my details from the other one.'

She looked at me quizzically, trying to pick out the identities.

'Thanks Cesc, that's helpful.'

'You know. The girl who got my number from the, from the first woman who paid me.'

'Right,' she said, fiddling with an unlit cigarette. 'And what? She paid you to let her beat you up.'

'Sort of. She was into some, well, relatively heavy stuff. And she had quite a lot of kit.'

'I thought it was men who paid women for that sort of stuff.'

'Well so did I. But she paid up. She did some quite painful things though. I think I was worth it.'

'Right. You really are a pervert, Cesc.'

'That's unfair. This was strictly professional.'

But Celeste, in a way, had a point. Although being singed and having your testicles tied to the ceiling is painful and really rather surprising, I'm fairly sure that I've done other things just as strange for no financial reward. Perhaps not quite as painful. But despite her protestations, I also had my fun. I suspect that she might have been letting me have a little reward, and that our activities could become progressively more extreme.

As my mind wandered, I heard myself asking Celeste, 'Do you know if sexual injuries are covered by insurance?'

She paused midway through a sip of her coffee.

'You've gone mad. All that testosterone has wiped your brain. You're the first person ever to be mentally afflicted by excessive sex.'

'I'm sure neither half of that is true.'

As I thought about it, I did realise the contradiction. The raven-haired woman had paid me a not insignificant sum of money to dish out something that many men would very happily have paid the same if not more to receive. Given all her kit, I even wondered if it might be one of those hobbies that balanced itself out: for every one of me, there was an equivalent client. She was certainly professional in her approach, if you can apply those terms to consensual sexual tortures.

What was more: I'd actually really enjoyed myself and was extremely glad I hadn't chosen the vanilla door, or whatever she called it. Sex is about intense sensations, and these were certainly that. There is no pleasure without pain, and in some circumstances, it seemed, raising the pain raised the pleasure. Although I didn't imagine that all my sexual encounters should necessarily be quite so, well, unique.

'Are you going to see her again?' asked Celeste.

'Yes. Same time next week.'

'Is she paying you again?'

'So it would seem.'

And the curious thing was, I would certainly have gone back for free. Despite the age gap, she was striking, and clearly loved sex, albeit in a fairly novel form. A lot of men would have been put off by having to put themselves in such a vulnerable position, or simply by the pain. It didn't bother me, and the thought of her underneath or towering over me turned me on enormously.

'What about the other one?' asked Celeste, interrupting my daydreaming.

'What about her?'

'Are you seeing her again?'

'Yes. I think so. It's slightly more complicated, as technically I'm seeking work, and, also technically, she's sort of responsible for supervising that entire aspect of the local economy. But I don't think it will be a problem. I need to get a real job, anyway. I can't keep signing on for ever, it's depressing.'

'So much so it's accentuated your sex problems,' she said.

'Thanks. You're all heart. Anyway, if I get many more assignments, I can sign myself off, as I won't need the money.'

'Won't they get suspicious?'

'No. I think I can probably claim that some friends of the family are helping me out. Or something like that.'

Celeste nodded.

'So you've had two clients so far?'

'Yes.'

'Both possible regulars?'

'Christ, you seem to know the terminology. Are you sure there's not something you aren't telling me?'

She said nothing.

'Yes,' I said, eventually, in the face of her chilly silence. 'Both may well become regulars.'

She thought for a while.

'Why,' I asked, after another odd pause.

'Oh, nothing,' she said.

Celeste seemed to lose her train of thought, and we talked about nothing in particular for a while before ordering some more coffee and then wandering back to the flat. I was lounging around with a book while Celeste dolled herself up for another date, when she poked her semi made-up face, her hair still half in curlers, around the door.

'Why don't you become a gigolo?' she asked. I sat up and pulled a face.

'A what?'

'A gigolo.'

'Because we're not in the 1970s,' I answered.

'So?'

It was, after all, my friend Celeste who suggested that I go professional.

'Seriously. Why don't you become a gigolo?' she continued. 'You do all the work. You've started charging. You may as well turn it into a profession.'

I was offended at first. But once she'd popped her head back behind the door, and left me to stew on the sofa, it started to make sense.

It was one thing having lots of sex, generally with more or less unknown girls I'd met through a variety of contacts. And it was another accepting money to sleep with people you don't particularly fancy. And it was a step even further to turn this into a profession. But it didn't seem quite as ridiculous as I might have thought a month or so earlier.

By the way, I should make something clear, just so you're not disappointed later: I'm not secretly in love with Celeste. I'm pretty sure she's not secretly in love with me. We take the piss out of each other a lot, and we even flirt, but we are seldom mistaken for a couple, and most of our friends would be absolutely shocked, possibly even appalled, if our flat-share turned into co-habitation. So, I can say now that we are not going to get together.

Part of it, I guess, is that we both know almost exactly where the other one has been. If not knowing can be off-putting, knowing, particularly in the amount of detail we both do, is definitely not conducive to a relationship. And although I only tease her about it, I'm pretty sure she sleeps with guys for money, or at least sleeps with people who can help her out financially and professionally. I imagine she probably does so in the same kind of bored and slightly insouciant fashion that she does everything else. So if we did end up together, it would lead to a strange financial stalemate, or the professional equivalent of a bread sandwich.

Chapter Twenty-two

I saw the raven-haired woman the next week, for another session of what amounted to complicated, occasionally violent and, particularly for me, dangerous sex. In a moment of something like respite, I realised that I did have to ask: what would have happened if I'd chosen the other door.

She had unzipped the hood she'd put over me, leaving my arms still uncomfortably strapped cruciform across the top of the iron frame.

'Seriously,' I gasped. 'What would have happened?'

She smiled, looking up from sucking my cock.

'An hour or so of vanilla sex, and then goodbye.'

'Right,' I said, leaning back and enjoying her mouth around me. Then, the sensation changed. I felt her grab a handful of my pubic hair, and then pull sharply. I screamed in pain.

'You're a lucky man,' she added, going back to sucking me.

She became my second regular.

The point was, despite the risk to my own well-being, with her, I would do it for free. It had even crossed my mind to ask whether we could have a session or two on my terms, without the money. But I realised that it would sound ridiculous and unprofessional. She did not want a lover. She wanted a paid partner.

I also thought about the effect of the money. On each occasion, she'd made sure that the matter of payment was sorted out beforehand. I had the option of taking the money and running, if I wanted to. It was clearly an important part of the ceremony to her. I didn't know whether she was rich or not, although the flat suggested that she had both money and good, if rather chilly, taste.

Paying seemed to relax her, in a way. Once that was sorted out, once the terms of the arrangement, including what amounted to any get-out clauses, were sorted, she was able to dedicate herself wholly to pleasure. Paying, in a way, made her able to express herself without worrying about offending or creating the wrong impression. If you asked an unpaid stranger to put on a funnel-shaped gag, they might raise their eyebrows and politely leave, even if they'd given the impression that they were into the same activities as you. But once you were paying, the rules of the game were pretty clear. Anything goes. The money meant that she could do pretty much what she pleased, and she didn't have to ask anyone's permission, or worry about hurting anyone's feelings. My testicles, I'll admit, were another matter altogether.

After another session with the raven-haired woman, my first Jenny – J. – called to arrange another meeting. I agreed, and saw her again, for the same price. The sex was energetic and extremely satisfying. We were both more relaxed than the time before, and although I was just as focused on her pleasure, I already knew a lot of the buttons to push, and so was able to try things out on her. I discovered that she was particularly keen on having sex standing up. We found a position where she sat on my thighs as I stood, with her reaching up to hold the doorframe, legs wrapped round my waist as I massaged her buttocks and sucked on her tits. She came like that, her hair whipping my face, bouncing up and down on my thighs, before we fell panting down to the floor.

Sometime later, once we'd finished, I told J. of my

decision.

'I'm thinking very seriously about making this into a profession. Can you help?'

She laughed.

'Why? Because I work in HR?'

'I guess so. Can you?'

She stood up, still naked, and looked for a packet of cigarettes.

'You smoke?' she asked.

'Only passively. And quite a lot.'

I thought briefly about mentioning that as this was my place of work, I should ask her not to spark up. But I changed my mind once I realised just how stupid it would sound.

She came back and sat next to me. She lit a cigarette and took a few drags. 'All the other guys I've paid to be with have been escorts.'

'Escorts?'

'Yeah. They're a mix of strippers, bouncers and students, generally, and they get in with an agency. The agency promises them big bucks for sex. They make some money, but as they're doing something that's basically illegal, they get ripped off.'

'I guess that's always the way with prostitution.'

She nodded.

'I guess the trick is to be your own boss,' she said.

'When you say it's illegal ...?'

'Well, it's unlikely that if you accept money for sex you're ever going to go to jail. But if you do anything that could be seen as soliciting, like overtly offering your services, you're in trouble. Or anything that could be a disturbance of the peace, say offering your wares on a street corner.'

'Right. Hey, I'm glad I asked you.'

'You're welcome,' she said. 'If I was in your position, I'd set up as an independent escort. Put out some ads, the women will know the drill. You'll barely have to mention it.'

'And on the plus side, I may even get some real escort work.'

'Plus side?' she asked.

'I take your point. What,' I said, lazily flicking her nipple with a finger, 'could be better work than this?'

'Exactly,' she said, sliding her hand up the length of my once-more hard cock.

Chapter Twenty-three

J. was a perfect customer.

She was regular, discreet and wealthy. She paid up on time, and she was able to help me out in surprising ways. On the few occasions we saw each other in public, she gave not the merest hint that we knew each other. On one occasion, when we chanced across each other with a mutual friend in a pub in Angel, she even acted the flirtatious stranger. When we were together, she told me exactly what she wanted, and gave enough clues the rest of the time so that my guesses were almost always spot on.

From a professional point of view, she was also a brilliant contact. She told me what to do to work as an escort, and gave me some good pointers to avoid getting arrested for soliciting or tax evasion. Apparently, both are very common in this profession, along with petty theft and breaking and entering.

I got a very strong impression that she knew rather a lot about the sex trade, possibly as a customer, but quite possibly also as an ex-provider. Financially, she seemed to have not only a very well-paid job, but also other mysterious sources of income. Occasionally she would let slip details of one work project or another, details which I generally forgot after her second or third orgasm.

Her job also helped me a lot. I found out that she was some sort of super-consultant, hired via a private contractor at remarkable fees to carry out innovative projects apparently designed to make everyone's working lives more difficult. This meant that she basically ran her own life and everyone else's with a surprising combination of responsibility and freedom. I suspect that the paid sex was a simple way of letting off steam.

She also helped me sort things out regarding my failed job seeking. She spoke to some people, I stopped showing up, they stopped paying me and nothing more was said. I wasn't sent on any chain gangs or made to accept menial jobs, and although, obviously, the dole cheques stopped coming, I only needed to pull a few sessions a week to earn more than I'd ever done as a barman or a failed actor. With time, and a steady increase in clients, it became a lucrative line.

My first few clients were all down to J. A few days after my second or third assignment with her, my mobile rang. The number was withheld, and I got a feeling that I knew what it was going to be about. Clearly J. had been sharing the line, because the voice on the other end said without so much as a hello, 'Is that Cesc? I hear you're great in bed and fuck for money.'

I liked the additional compliment.

'Who's that?'

'Let's say I'm a friend of a friend. Are you looking for some work?'

'I'm always looking for work,' I answered.

'What are you like at giving head?'

'Some women moan a bit,' I said, 'but that's the only complaint I ever get.'

'A comedian, too.'

'No. Just an escort,' I said.

'What are you doing tomorrow night?'

'You,' I said.

I told her the conditions, and she gave me an address.

'Good. I'll see you then.'

As I prepared, I thought about the voice: she sounded much younger than the other women, and despite the cockiness, there was a certain naivety in her tone. She didn't sound like the type of wealthy female libertine, sexual explorer or busy career woman who I'd thought would be my most likely customer.

I took a taxi and turned up a couple of minutes early. There were a number of things that were new. Firstly, the flat smacked neither of wealth nor social clout: we were in a semi-salubrious district of north London, nowhere near a tube line. From outside, the house looked neat and new, divided up into smallish conversions. The third floor, which I believed to be her flat, had the lights on and tidy window boxes. It's always good, I reflected, to have a well-trimmed bush to display when you're expecting company.

After double-checking the address, I buzzed. The door opened, and I stepped inside. The stairs were narrow and tight, and I eventually found myself outside the flat door. It had a cheery, hand-painted letter on it. I knocked, noticing as I did that outside there was post addressed to two people. I wondered whether it might be a set-up.

The door opened, and I was greeted by a small, pretty girl, my age or possibly even less, with a short bob of hair, like something out of a Goddard movie. I clocked immediately a male presence in the flat: shoes, sports kit, lots of CDs. I now knew it was a set-up. I also noticed, on her very small hands, an engagement ring. I said nothing, just smiled and accepted her offer to come inside.

'Would you like a drink?' she offered, walking away from me into a small but airy living room.

'Thanks.'

'We have some whisky. Or I'm drinking wine.' She gave a nervous titter. I studied her more closely: she was short, almost elfin, with almond eyes. Everything about her was petite and delicate. I immediately imagined the type of fun she'd be looking for.

'Wine is fine, if that's what you're having. I don't think I got your name.'

'You can call me Sophie, if you like.'

'OK, Sophie. Have you done this sort of thing before?'

'I'll get you that drink. Make yourself at home.'

I sat down on a throw-covered futon, noticing a large pair of trainers and a baseball bat. I was excited by the job, but also slightly perturbed by the possibility of violent retribution. I wanted my career to last more than two clients.

As she returned, I avoided the subject of the phantom fiancé.

'I know you're wondering,' she said. 'You're obviously far too professional to ask.'

'Ask what?' I replied.

'My fiancé. He's away.'

'It's OK. I'm a professional. I'm only here for one thing, and that's you. Everything else is just background noise.'

'Can I tell you something though, before we, you know, before we start?'

'It's OK. Don't be nervous,' I said.

'Of course. Silly. Look, I'll be honest. I'm engaged.'

'You said.'

'I've never had an orgasm with a guy.'

'It happens,' I said quietly.

'I've been with him for three years. And I've never come. I've never come with any man.'

102

'And with yourself?'

'Yes. Quite a lot, in fact.'

'OK,' I said, thinking to myself. 'How would you normally do it?'

'God. I can't believe I'm having this conversation.' She thought for a few seconds. 'In the bath?' she said, or rather asked.

'You know what they say, don't you?'

'What,' she replied.

'Sixty per cent of women admit they masturbate. And forty per cent think that everyone really believes they take that long in the shower.'

She giggled.

'And do you use anything? Do you have a vibrator?'

'I have one. But I don't use it in the bath. I'd be electrocuted.'

I laughed. 'OK. I think this is something that can be remedied.'

I reached my hand out and held hers. I lifted it to my lips and kissed the palm. Then I ran the back of the palm across her cheek, and ran it up the nape of her neck, through her hair, as I kissed her cheek, and the corner of her mouth.

'Where's your bathroom?' I said, pulling back.

'Through there,' she answered, looking slightly surprised.

'I'll be back.'

I went through and found what I call the masturbator's bathroom: small, but with a wide, deep tub, surrounded by sponges and tons of different gels and oils. I ran the water and poured in what smelt like the most arousing of scents. With the water running, I returned to her. She had barely moved from where I had left her.

103

'We can take our time. I'm really quite looking forward to this.'

'I'm not going to carry on faking it. I want to know what's the problem,' she said, apparently continuing a conversation she'd been having in her head.

'Normally, the problem is patience. We have a saying in Argentina. An elephant can fuck an ant, but he needs two things. One is patience.'

'What's the other?' she asked.

'Saliva,' I said.

I kissed her again, only briefly, and then lifted her towards me. I perched her in front of me, facing away, between my legs, and began to massage her back and shoulders.

'Mmm. That's nice,' she said.

Very slowly, as I kneaded her slim shoulders, I slipped down the straps of her dress. I moved round and gently ran the back of my hands down her breasts. I carried on working light circles with my fingertips, and then slipped the dress off fully. I helped her to her feet, and the dress fell off. Underneath, she was wearing nothing but a small pair of panties. I moved her round so that she was lying back down on the sofa, and began to kiss and lick her small breasts. She arched her back and closed her eyes in pleasure.

'Oh, I like that,' she said.

I kissed my way down her abdomen, and then took the top of her knickers in my teeth. I very slowly peeled them down over her smooth pubis. A thin line of wispy hair was all she had left from her last wax job.

'You're a very sexy little thing, you know,' I said.

With her naked, I picked her up from the sofa. I held her tight and with my lower hand gently moved towards her pussy.

'Come on,' I said, and carried her away.

In the bathroom, the water was hot and deep. I helped her in and stood back.

'Now,' I said. 'Show me what you do.'

She was already enjoying herself and clearly excited. I saw her reach down without a word and begin to stroke herself. Meanwhile, I undressed. Through half-closed eyes she looked at my erection while playing with herself under the water.

'This isn't fair,' she whispered. 'You're not doing anything.'

I walked towards her and slid into the bath behind her. My cock nestled between her buttocks, and I ran it along her thighs.

'Stand up,' I said. She stood. I slid down into the bath, bubbles around my head. 'Now sit down,' I said.

She sat, placing her small, neat pussy just close to my tongue. I put my hands behind my head to prevent drowning, and then stretched my tongue to meet her.

'You can forget I'm here, if you like,' I said.

'I've got a better idea,' she said.

She unwrapped the condom I'd left on the side of the bath and slipped it onto me. Soon she was sucking my cock enthusiastically while I worked my tongue against her clit. Meanwhile, I freed a hand and began to finger her, gently at first, and then deeper and more firmly, while I increased the rhythm and force of my tongue strokes. She stopped sucking and began to moan with pleasure.

'Oh God. I'm so close,' she said.

I slowed my strokes to slow, insistent licks, tasting her juice and sliding a second finger into her tight pussy. She gasped and continued her encouragement, now holding my cock firmly in her little hand.

'Oh yes, now, please. Yes,' she said.

I sped up with my tongue while she began to pull her nipples hard, riding up and down, steadying herself with the other hand. Her buttocks and stomach were tensing and relaxing, and I could tell that she was very close. Suddenly, I withdrew my tongue.

'Oh no. What's wrong?' she said, with a look of alarm on her face.

'Nothing's wrong,' I said. I pushed her upwards and then helped her turn around. 'I hope you're ready,' I said. She was panting and almost trembling. Very ready, I thought. I lowered her slowly onto me. My cock entered her only partially, but with a twist I found myself right inside her. She groaned as I leant back, exposing her clit for me to play with. I teased it with my thumb and forefinger before starting a steady rhythm against it. She pulled on her nipples and rode me. The water splashed around us, and the expression on her face was close to pain.

'Oh yes. Please. Don't stop now,' she shouted. I continued to help her ride me while maintaining the rhythm and pressure on her clit. She moved from words to shrill shrieks and groans. 'I'm so near,' she managed to whisper.

I continued with hands and cock; it took three, possibly five more minutes for her orgasm to begin. Her groans became moans, which became little cries and gasps. Once she had begun to take sobbing gulps of air, I knew that she was coming properly. From short sharp bounces she changed to leaping arcs, drawing my cock almost out and then deep within her, water splashing all around us. With one final thrust she was finished, collapsing almost weeping onto my chest.

'That was amazing,' she said.

'That was just the start,' I said. She sat up slightly, and I spun her around, my cock still deep inside. On my lap she rocked back and forth, my penis deeper inside and at a different angle. I played with her clit and nipples, and she came a second time within seconds. The third took longer, but was the biggest and most intense of them all. I also decided to come, and as she released her desperate flutters, I felt myself throb and pulsate deep within her, before we both collapsed back down into the water.

We spent a minute or two lying in the water. Once her breathing had calmed down, she whispered a few words of approval and then stepped out of the water. I followed her, and we towelled down.

'That's the first time I've ever come with a guy,' she said, ruffling the back of her hair with a towel.

'I hope you enjoyed it.'

She stepped towards me and reached up to give me a kiss.

'It was amazing,' she said. 'Let's do it again.'

We went through into the bedroom where I got a proper chance to look at her naked. She lay stretched on the bed, slim and taught. I went down on her, sliding my tongue gently into her, then deeper, and then licking her clit and savouring her taste. Her smooth skin turned me on and I felt my cock rigid against the sheets. She came again, quickly and more quietly this time, grabbing my hair and pushing me into her pussy, before I sat back up and turned her onto all fours. She moaned with pleasure as I slid into her.

She was an enthusiastic partner, urging me to thrust harder and deeper, noisily expressing herself as she came. The quivers inside her aroused me and soon I was coming again, clasping her around her slim waist and

107

drawing her towards me.

Later, we lay together, naked on the bed.

'Do you mind if I smoke?' she said.

'Do you smoke?' I said.

'No. But I think I probably should. Is it always like that?'

'Sometimes. I must say that even in a professional capacity, that was very enjoyable.'

She laughed. 'It's never been like that before. Not even when I've, you know …'

'Done it yourself?'

She giggled. 'Yes.'

'It's just a question of patience.'

'But some women never come.'

'I've not met any. Or at least not that I've known.'

She looked at me, propping her chin on her hand.

'Why are you a gigolo, Cesc?' she asked.

'Well I'm not. Not really. I'm relatively new to this.'

'Really?' she said. 'You seem very professional.'

'I was a committed amateur for a long time.'

She laughed again. After a while, idly running a hand along her flank, I spoke.

'Like a lot of things. For the money. I got into it a bit by accident. I'm really only starting up. I think in the eyes of the law I have to call myself an escort.'

'You can escort me all you like,' she said, half cringing to herself.

'Do you want me to see you again?' I asked.

'It's tricky. Yes. I'd like to. I need to make sure my fiancé's away.'

'You should make him try harder. You deserve it. And by the way, using a vibrator during sex is perfectly fair game too.'

'OK.' She looked at the clock: we'd been there for a

lot longer than I'd imagined. 'You should go, though.
I'm sorry.'

'Don't apologise. The customer's always right,' I
said.

Although I didn't see her as often as the others,
'Sophie' became the third client on my growing list.

Chapter Twenty-four

With three clients, I felt capable of setting up something like a business. Maybe 'outfit' is better. I've never had much of a head for business, but luckily I had some good advice. J. pointed me in the direction of some listings mags, and Celeste took it upon herself to tell a few people she knew who might be interested.

I also learnt the lessons of my experience Internet dating. I deleted the various profiles that I had on contact sites, and instead focused my attention on one website that elegantly skirted around the fact that it was effectively a forum for offering sex for money. I thought about image: I wanted to make it clear that I offered great sex to women who wanted it; I wasn't a stripper, I wasn't some sort of disciplinarian and I didn't go with men.

J. pointed out a few things about the financial side: it might look odd that I was paying rent, buying clothes, indeed eating and living without any discernible income. I had two options, she suggested. Either disappear and reappear under an assumed name (apparently this is relatively easy and happens a lot, certainly in the world of business and particularly in businesses related to matters sexual), or run something relatively legit, 'admit' what I earned from that, and pay tax.

I've never been a great one for tax, and the thought of giving a percentage of my clients' fuck money to the government seemed strange. But given a choice between screwing for money and paying tax, or being screwed in the butt to stay alive in jail, I chose the sensible option. At the same time, it was also clear that, like taxi drivers who live in mansions in Epping but admit to earning only £8K a year, my escort business did not need to be particularly lucrative.

The other good thing about the profession was the freebies: dinners out, occasional gifts and, of course, the little number I had going on free clothes. Most of my dates were local, and occasionally I'd even get picked up. Rich women can be very generous. And I noticed that as the business developed, the women seemed to get wealthier. Wealthier, and increasingly decadent.

So, technically, in the eyes of the law, and as far as the adverts I post seem to say, I am an escort. I have set up as a business, and any income on those activities is taxable. I don't solicit: it is almost always the woman who asks. Sometimes escort work turns into call-guying, sometimes it doesn't. But you won't find me on a street corner, and I don't go cold calling.

It wasn't all simple at first. One of my first problems was the name. Cesc Aleixandre is a hell of a mouthful. Although it sounds suitably exotic for the job, it brings a whole series of problems. Firstly, no one can pronounce it, particularly not the first few clients. After a couple of weeks, I got a call:

'Hi. Is that Cisco,' said a voice that reeked of smoke and excess.

'Yes, that's me. It's Cesc.'

'Ah, Kesc, sorry.'

'No, don't worry, everyone gets it wrong.'

Curiously, that girl had a particular talent for getting it wrong. When we met, she greeted me as Chesc. I corrected her again, and she apologised, but I realised that it was becoming faintly awkward. I didn't even try telling her my surname. She was independently wealthy, tall, formerly married to a banker, slightly horsy looking, and, I soon found out, a frustrated pervert who with my help became a former frustrated pervert. Let's call her Virginia, or V.

During our first session, V. called me 'Fran', 'Chesc', and 'Kesc'. As she was coming, she used another name altogether, which I could barely make out through the silk scarf she'd had me knot in her mouth, but, if memory served, I discovered later to be that of one of her dogs.

I thought long and hard about how to make my name pronounceable and memorable. Celeste advised that I change it, offering a series of increasingly ridiculous names.

'What about Dick Wood?' she suggested.

'I'm not a porn star,' I answered.

'So? How about Max Hardman?'

'Look, that's ridiculous. I'm not some steroid-pumped Viagra-popping American. I need something that suggests a bit of class and discernment. Which my own name does perfectly well.'

'But what good is that if no one can say it or remember it?'

'Well maybe once they've shouted it out in orgasmic reverie a few times, they should remember.'

'Ahh,' said Celeste, puffing on her cigarette and trying to get the attention of a waiter inside, before giving up and flicking her ash onto the table, 'that's the problem though, isn't it. What if you don't get that far? What if they don't hire you? Because you have a silly name.'

I gave her a dirty look, but had to admit there was some sense in her argument. That week another client called. Before we'd even got down to discussing the details of the assignment, she was questioning me about the name.

'Where's it from?'

'It's kind of Spanish,' I said.

'Kind of?' she asked.

'Yes. It's a long story. I can tell you later, if you really like.'

'Well later I think we'll have better things to do, don't you think?'

So I started telling her about my family, but after a few moments I realised that I was boring her. I tried to return to the matter of the assignment, but it was clear that in the few seconds I'd wasted she'd changed her mind. She made some sort of half-baked excuse to put me on hold, and then cut me off. I rang back, but the phone was off. I never like looking desperate, so I left it at that. I realised that my name had lost me a pay cheque.

'This is serious, Celeste,' I said to her later, at the flat.

'What is?'

'I lost a client because of my name.'

'Really? I did warn you. So are you going to change it? I've thought of a really good one.'

I gave a look that I hoped would make it clear that I wasn't in the market for a fake moniker. But she carried on regardless.

'Here. It's perfect. You should call yourself "Ace McFuck".'

'Celeste, that's not even a name. None of the elements of it are a name.'

'Mc is a name,' she said, with a shrug. 'And I've got a friend called Ace.'

'I've met him. His name is Alistair. And he's a twat.'

'You're so ungrateful. I'm just trying to help your career.'

'I'm not calling myself Ace McFuck.'

'Is it because you don't like the Scottish? Are you being racist? You know my Dad is Scottish?'

'No. No. And yes, I do.'

'So Ace Fuck then?'

'No,' I said, trying not to shout at her. She was clearly enjoying my predicament far too much.

The answer came a few weeks later, with V.

'Tell me about your name,' she said, lounging on a thick rug in front of the fire in one of the living rooms in her Maida Vale town house. It was one of three properties she keeps in the city, this one being dedicated to her arty projects and business ventures. And, it seemed, to the pursuit of sex.

We'd just finished an acrobatic session trying out a series of sex toys that she'd been importing. It turned out she'd been using some of her vast fortune to start an erotic emporium for discerning ladies who know. She obviously didn't need the money, but it was at least something she had a real interest in, or least seemed to, given her reaction to my use of a vibrating jade cock-ring imported from Japan.

'Why not tell me about yours?' I said.

'Mine's boring. Very ordinary. Besides, it's false, of course. Yours has something exotic, yet true, about it.'

I tried to avoid taking the mickey out of her rather over-the-top analyses, and instead explained briefly the complicated story of my family history, and the source of a name that sounds foreign pretty much anywhere. I kept it brief: she was a busy woman who bored easily; I'd also learnt my lesson from the previous case of the lost client. I also mentioned the problem that I had with no one being able to pronounce or remember it.

'Is that a problem? I mean you're not being hired for

114

conversation,' she said.

I felt, very briefly, insulted, before realising that it was an odd sort of compliment.

'Well, technically I'm an escort. So you could hire me for a chat.'

'Like a therapist,' she suggested.

'Yes. But you're right. I don't get hired for the talk. The problem is it doesn't really help the marketing.'

'Quite the young entrepreneur, aren't you,' she said, half mocking.

'Everyone has to take care of business, no?'

She nodded.

'How is it pronounced again?' she asked.

'Cesc,' I said, stressing the s sounds.

'Hmm. Ssessk,' she said. 'You need a lot of tongue for that. No wonder you're so good at what you do.'

'Thanks.'

'You know it sounds a bit like Sex.'

I looked at her.

'You're a genius. That's it.'

'You're welcome. Now, go and put that tongue to work, will you.'

It was the least I could do.

The Joy of Cesc, I thought.

Chapter Twenty-five

Back at the flat, I talked about it with Celeste. I told her about the conversation with V.

'That's the horsy one, right?' she said.

'Don't call her that. And don't tell anyone I called her that. I don't want anyone to think I talk about clients in disrespectful terms.'

'Right. But you do though. Quite a lot,' Celeste said.

'That's not true. I'm not as bad as you, anyway.'

'Look, forget it. What about the name?'

'She said it sounded like Sex.'

'Well you certainly smell like it,' Celeste said.

'It's just my natural pheromones,' I replied.

'Bullshit. Anyway, you need something like a tag line,' Celeste said. 'Something unique, something to brand you.'

'To brand me? That sounds painful. Have you been reading *The Story of O* again?' I asked.

'You know I hate that book. It was the worst present you ever bought me.'

'You're so ungrateful.'

'Sounds like Sex. Well I suppose it does a bit.' She pondered my name and its sound for a few seconds. 'Sounds like Sex would be quite a cool name,' she suggested, after a while.

'I've got something better,' I said.

'Really? What?'

'Wait for it … *The Joy of Cesc.*'

'Hmm,' said Celeste, apparently unconvinced.

'It's a great name for a call guy service, don't you think?'

She seemed to warm to the idea.

'I'll admit that, for once, it's not a totally stupid idea. Good work, Cesc. I mean, you need something that will make you instantly memorable. And, I guess, it solves the problem of no one knowing how to pronounce your name.'

So it was settled. I opened a web page with that name, as well as changing my profile on the contact website. It seemed to work. The next couple of calls both got my name right, and both led to what I call passing trade: one-night sessions of paid pleasure that don't turn into a regular deal.

In the meantime, Celeste seemed to be taking far too much interest in my work. A few days later, we were chatting in the living room of the flat. I was getting ready for a date with the raven-haired woman, or Raven, as I'd started to call her on my phone and in my diary. She'd asked me to wear leather, and I was sitting awkwardly on the sofa in a pair of trousers that had cut off the blood supply to my feet.

'By the way,' Celeste said. 'I had an idea.'

'What?'

'You need cards.'

'Cards?'

'Like business cards. Calling cards. It gives a touch of class.'

'Really?'

She showed me a few samples that a friend of hers printed. I had to admit that they did have an elegant feel to them: thick paper, embossed black ink, and not the sort of thing someone would tear up to use as a filter in a roll-up.

'I could go for that,' I said.

I paid Celeste to have some cards made up. A few

days later, she was back with a slim metal case, containing a deck of business cards.

'What do you think?'

'I'm not sure about this. Isn't it going a bit far?'

'Going further than sleeping with women for money?'

'We almost never,' I said, 'sleep.'

'Just look at the card, Cesc,' she said.

I took a look at the card.

> ### *The Joy of Cesc*

On the back was my mobile number.

It was, as promised, a white card with black embossed lettering. I thought it looked a little bit tacky.

'You're a gigolo, Cesc, what do you expect?'

'I'm not a gigolo.'

'What are you, then?'

'I don't know. But that's not the word. Certainly as far as the law is concerned, I'm an escort.'

'Look, don't be so picky. I think they're perfect.'

I wasn't convinced, but I decided to give them a try. I gave a few to J., a couple more to Raven and a handful to V. I didn't let Sophie have any, as I was worried her fiancé might pick them up. Also, I felt rather odd using a girl I in fact quite liked to pick up more trade. I handed over a couple at an erotica shop I knew, where I'd bought a few tools of the trade in the early weeks of my enterprise. I was pleasantly surprised when the cards started to pay off.

Chapter Twenty-six

The first success came after a session with Raven. I was undoing some twine that was about to cut through the flesh on my wrists having just play-forced her to swallow me through a weird gag-like contraption. Where, I wondered, did she get these marvellous toys?

After she had unstrapped the device, and I had freed my hands, she mentioned the business cards.

'I have a friend. I gave her a card. I think she might be interested.'

'Great. What sort of stuff is she in to?'

'Oh, she's much, much, weirder than me.'

'Really?'

'Much weirder.'

'Yes?'

'Oh yes. Occasionally,' she said, leaning towards me and running her hands up my thighs, 'I even have very normal sex.'

To prove it, she held my cock while running a finger down to her clit. She kept her pussy trimmed short, but in a low wide triangle. She'd told me it was because men who didn't like pubic hair weren't really looking for women. I didn't disagree, but only out of politeness. The advantage, I've always thought, of a shaven pubis is simply ease of access, particularly for oral.

Soon we were in a sixty-nine position, her pussy stationed over my tongue, my cock deep into her mouth. She came once, almost biting my cock, before I slid out from under her, slipped on one of the studded condoms that she liked and entered her slowly on all fours. What she called 'normal' sex was noisy and energetic, but for once there was no beating or binding. Simply, I fucked her steadily and hard, reaching around to massage her clit and with the other hand to tease and tweak her breasts. With her height, it was a good position; we fitted firmly together, and with her ankles over mine I could achieve deep penetration that satisfied us both. I carried on my thrusts until she reached another orgasm, and just to reassert normality, I came inside her, with no spectacular displays of mock humiliations.

'So tell me about your friend. She sounds like a pervert,' I said, as we lay post-coitus.

'We went to school together. She was a very naughty girl. Funnily enough, I had my first orgasm with her.'

'Really? Sex or masturbation?'

'Oh, sex, of course.'

'That's good to know. You must like sharing things,' I said, hoping to make it clear that a threesome was definitely an option I would accept.

'Yes. Anyway, she'll give you a call.'

True to her word, Raven's friend called.

'Is that Cesc?' she asked.

'Yes, it's me.'

'Is there anything you won't do for money?'

'Animals and children. And probably non-consenting third parties. But I wouldn't want to place too many limits, you know.'

'Good. My friend tells me you're good.'

'That's nice to hear. Customer feedback, and all that.'

There was a quiet, contained laugh.

'I'd like to meet somewhere public. I know a bar.'

She gave me some details – I'd never heard of the place but it sounded expensive. I couldn't quite work out the reason for the public meeting, but it was on her time, so all the better.

Later, I noticed a pattern that emerged: the cards attracted women who were looking to try out a particular sexual fantasy. Or, occasionally, a series of them. But Raven's friend was the first, and, in many ways, the one who made the strongest impression.

I took a taxi down into town that evening and stepped out onto the steps of a private club off Charlotte Street. A statuesque Polish blonde who could have walked straight off a modelling shoot welcomed me, took my coat, and showed me through, sashaying deliciously in what was clearly an attempt to arouse customers into excessive purchases of ridiculously overpriced vodka and champagne. Inside, the joint was darkly lit and decked out mostly in red: velvet, leather booths and a long bar made almost entirely of mirrors.

Raven's friend was waiting for me in a corner booth, out of the way, but not hiding. She was Raven's age, obviously, with fine cheekbones and long bleached hair tied loosely back. She was dressed for the office, but with a suit whose cut suggested the work of a samurai, not a tailor. She was sexy, but also, very slightly frightening. I was looking forward to it.

'Hi. I'm Cesc, pleased to meet you,' I said, extending a hand. She took it.

'I'm Julia,' she said, and as she shook my hand I noticed the other one: it had a silver ring around her middle finger with a leather strap that stretched back to a wrist cuff.

'I like your jewellery,' I said.

'Thank you. Sit down.'

I sat.

She ordered a drink, vodka, straight up, and ordered me the same thing without asking.

'Nice place you've got here,' I said, sipping the drink.

The alcohol went straight up my nose, and for a second I worried that my head might catch fire.

'It's a little club, really, a friend of mine runs it.'

I couldn't help but notice that to go with the Polish beauty on the door there was a stunning Japanese waitress in skin-tight silk, as well as a barman who'd clearly been dropped in from a Gucci ad. I started to guess the type of place it might be.

'I have a room here. Would you like to see it?'

'Very much so.'

We necked our drinks and I followed her into a small, silver elevator at the back of the bar. On the landing, two or three floors up, were striking prints in bold reds and neons of painted nudes, many in acrobatic poses or against scenes of natural beauty. I could feel an erection coming on already.

She opened the room with a large iron key. As she went in, I got a chance to admire her figure. Above her stilettos were perfectly turned ankles, and her skirt was dangerously short. She had clearly spent a long time looking after herself.

Inside, there was a large oval bed, a matching couch and a large baroque mirror, directly in front of the bed. The bed had an ornate wrought-iron frame; on closer inspection, it also had what looked like hooks. The only other ornamentation was a picture of a voluptuous model in a Westwood corset, adopting a particularly welcoming pose.

'Have you heard of depravation?' she asked, turning to me.

'Deprivation? Are you planning on locking me up?'

'No, depravation, I said.'

'Don't you mean depravity?'

'Not quite. It's a term we use.'

She paused for a moment, licking at an imaginary spot of gloss on her lips.

'My friend told me that you were good at following instructions, and that you were not put off by, let's say, certain more extreme forms of pleasure.'

'That's true. But she's not that extreme.'

'I need you to be.'

'OK.'

'I'm going to give you a series of instructions, and I want you to follow them. To the letter.'

'OK. That's clear.'

'They are written down, in that envelope. If you can do this correctly, you'll have a regular customer. I'll be in the other room.'

She went out through a door by the bed. I went over to the envelope that had been left on the bed and opened it. She was right. There was a series of instructions. And they were quite, well, extreme. For a second I thought about leaving, but decided that it would be cowardly. And, she was extremely sexy.

As the instructions pointed out, there was a drawer under the bed. I found the things that she mentioned she would need. I prepared them, as instructed. Then I checked my instructions again, trying to memorise the order. I could see what she meant by depravation. I looked at the last line again, not quite understanding its meaning:

'Don't worry. You can't hurt me.'

And then I began.

The door to the other room gave way with a crash, and I found her hiding in a corner. I grabbed her arm and her hair and pulled her up. She screamed at me, and tried to resist. I blocked the slap she threw at me with an arm, and caught that hand as well. She was tall and had good reach, but I was much stronger than her. I dragged her into the bedroom, and as she tried to kick me, I dodged, tripped her and pushed her to the floor. Following the impact I was able to pin her down.

The first item was a pair of cuffs. I bound her hands together, and then found the long leather strap, and ran it under the strap of her ring. I stood up over her and ran the strap around one of the legs of the bed frame. It pulled on her finger and on her wrists, and I could see pain in her expression. I found a blindfold and tied it tightly over her eyes. She began to swear and insult me, and shook and resisted as I tore at her clothes. With her blouse open I ripped off her bra, and then harshly pulled down her skirt. Her thong was under her suspenders, and I snapped it off from between her legs with a firmness and speed that made her wince.

With her dishevelled and bound on the floor, I found the next items: ankle cuffs. They fitted neatly round the straps on her stilettos, and then I bundled her onto the bed and strapped them to the bottom of the frame. With her still shouting at me, I left her for a second.

'You can't see me. You can't move. I can do anything to you,' I said, from across the room. And then from closer, 'and I will.'

I took one of the vibrators that she'd left and turned it on. I ran it over her chest and her nipples, but just as she began to express pleasure instead of fury, I quickly moved it to her mouth and pushed it in, further in than could be comfortable. She half gagged and I removed it, now dripping saliva. I ran it down her body, over her clit, used it to separate her lips and briefly slid the head in. She moaned with pleasure, and I gave her more. Then I turned it off.

'It sounds like you're enjoying that. I'll stop.'

I moved it away from her pussy, and then down. I pushed it between her buttocks. She made as if to resist, so I parted them with my fingers, and despite her efforts, slid the wet vibrator into her. She winced, and I pushed it further in, opening her up, despite her groans of discomfort. Then I stepped away from her. I could see that her nipples were hard.

'You're obviously enjoying this too much,' I said, to a foul-mouthed response. I found what looked like a pair of hairgrips, tweaked her nipples out, and then attached them. I pressed them tight, and then flicked the tips hard.

'Is it painful?' I said. 'Because I'm worried you're enjoying this.' While flicking her nipples, I reached down and began to stroke her clitoris. Her pussy was wet and clearly ready for me. But instructions are instructions.

After a few more minutes she was whimpering with alternate pleasure and pain, between each flick and each stroke, and I moved away and pushed the dildo further into her. I found another vibrator, with a clitoral stimulator on the top, set it on a slow setting and slid it into her. She gasped, but meanwhile I was preparing the next step.

I found what I was looking for: it was something like a face mask, but it had two plugs for the nostrils and a sort of removable mouthpiece or tube. Once in place, it seemed to enable you to control whether the wearer could breathe or not. As the twin vibrators did their jobs bringing her to greater and greater arousal, I attached the mask, placing it between her teeth and covering her nose.

As her breathing quickened, I covered the hole. She quivered and shook, with pleasure and perhaps discomfort, as the air supply was cut off and her approaching orgasm demanded heart-pumping effort. After a few seconds, I let her breathe again; she gasped, almost sobbing.

As her pleasure increased, I covered the air hole again, this time for slightly longer: her face began to take a ruby tone, and I could see her start to panic, her head turning from side to side, unable to free the air hole from my cover. I let her breathe again, and then turned off the vibrator. She tried to shout something at me, but could not because of the gag.

I stepped away and tightened the straps so that she was spread-eagled, vibrators still in place and nipples still squeezed tight. I took my time undressing and then ran my hard dick down her body and along her thighs, before slipping on one of Raven's condoms.

'I'm going to enjoy this,' I said. I removed the top vibrator and entered her, turning it back on and applying it to her clit. Her reaction was immediate: she curved her back and pulled against her bonds. But as her pleasure increased, I held my hand to her mouthpiece. Instead of arching with pleasure, she began to squirm underneath me. But tied up as she was, there was no way out. I continued to fuck her, with the vibrator buzzing against her clit, while she struggled for air. When I allowed her to breathe, she gasped for a noisy breath, and with it, broke into a rocking, pulsating orgasm.

Once she'd finished, I pulled out, replacing my penis with the vibrator. She began to come again, immediately, while I removed the mouthpiece from her gag. I pulled her head forward by the hair and found that my cock was almost a perfect fit for the hole as I slipped it in. I rocked back and forth, squatting over her, forcing my penis in and out. I savoured the orgasm, possibly for slightly too long, as when I pulled out, she spluttered desperately and choked down gasping gulps of air. I removed the vibrators and collapsed back on the bed.

'Because you've been good,' I said. 'I'm not going to punish you. But you should know, I could find you any time. And I won't always be as nice.'

I looked at her. She was breathing heavily, her body wet with sweat, her legs spread in front of me. I felt like another screw, but a script's a script.

I undid the clamps on her nipples, removed the gag and pulled up her blindfold. Her eyes were wet with tears and she coughed and hiccoughed, trying to get her breath back. I unbound her hands and then her feet, and she sat up in bed, casting off her ruined blouse to reveal breasts that were still pert, her nipples still pointy from their punishment.

'Is that depravation?' I asked.

Despite her messy state, she maintained a chilly composure.

'Something like it. I'm impressed at your ability to follow instructions. Have you ever acted?'

'Briefly. Unsuccessfully,' I said.

'Good.' She pushed a stray hair out of her face and wiped some mascara that had run in streaks down her face. 'Yes. It's a word we use; depravity, and sensory deprivation. Depravation. Clever, eh?'

'Yes. Erm, can I ask you why you like doing it that way? Isn't it a bit of a risk? What if I was a psychopath?'

'But you aren't. Although you cut it a bit fine towards the end.'

'Exactly. Don't you worry about putting yourself in those sorts of situations, for pleasure?'

'I own an insurance firm. I like to be able to control lack of control. To make risk safe.'

I obviously didn't look convinced.

'Did you see the fisheye?' she asked.

I looked around: like most hotel rooms, there was a fisheye.

'No,' I said. I stood up and tried to look through it. I could see nothing.

'It doesn't work,' I said.

'It's for looking in,' she said. 'If anything went wrong, if you did anything that exceeded or distorted my wishes, you would have lasted no more than a few seconds.'

I tried to avoid gulping. 'Right. We were being, what, monitored? There was someone at the door?'

'Yes. And someone else watching via CCTV, of course.'

I looked around and saw the camera for the first time. I can be very unobservant at times.

'So this is totally controlled?' I said, not knowing whether to feel frightened or relieved.

'There are people here I can trust,' she continued. 'I'm glad you're one of them.'

Julia, unlike her Raven-haired friend, never went in for vanilla sex. And she became a regular.

Although she was a generous employer and there was something satisfying about the power she pretended to allow me to exercise over her, I never became wholly comfortable with the set-up, particularly being watched by bouncers. And I wasn't sure I liked being made to act the torturer, even if the so-called 'torture' always ended in massive mutual orgasms.

Still, I said nothing. She was a woman who knew what she wanted, and knew how to get it. Call guys really can't go about calling their clients perverts, after all.

Chapter Twenty-seven

Julia's requests were quite particular, but not the strangest things I got asked.

I'd had a couple of assignments with a professional girl in her mid thirties. I think she worked in a bank near Oxford Street. Let's call her Z. She was tall and slim, with a body used to exercise; she had long, light brown hair which she normally tied conservatively back, but her suits always sexily hugged her figure and she wore sharp stilettos with little ankle straps like J.'s.

It started out as an escort job, in fact, as she hired me for a work do, where I was my smart and charming best before we parted with a chaste kiss. I must have made the right impression, because she hired me for a second, bedroom assignment, and then our third encounter was an evening meet, starting with drinks in town. We met in an old theatrical pub near Chinatown. It was a fairly quiet, midweek night, and we chatted quite amiably about not much.

After a couple of drinks we were getting quite cosy, and I suggested we could either go for dinner or, perhaps, have one for the road and then she might like to come back to my place, for the business end of the date. She agreed, and I bought her another G&T, after which she seemed at least tipsy.

We sat close to each other in the taxi, and soon her hand had fallen on my knee. I held it, and after a moment, we kissed. There was something like anger in her passion, and I almost had to hold her back from mounting me there and then. I'm no prude. I just think taxi drivers have enough of a job paying attention to what's going on without the distraction of seeing rampant professionals fucking in the rear-view mirror.

Back at mine, Celeste was out, and so I showed Z. through to the main room. She sat, her legs crossed, her foot moving back and forth. As I poured drinks, I could see her stocking tops up the slit of her skirt.

We had barely touched the drinks before we were making out again. Soon we were intertwined, her small but pert breasts revealed after I unbuttoned her blouse and slipped off her bra. She hitched her skirt up to reveal a pair of tiny, lace trim knickers over her suspenders. I slid my hand up her thigh and worked my finger towards her clit. She was hot and wet, and as I stroked her sex and toyed with her nipples, she moaned and began to bite my neck.

She came quickly, her juices running onto my fingers, which I put to her lips for her to taste. Then she reached down and freed my cock, before bending over to mouth it. She had fantastic technique, running her tongue up and down the length while sucking it deep into her mouth and using her lips to pleasure me.

I held off from coming and scrabbled around for a condom.

I should make a brief digression here: I always use condoms. It's a rule. If I don't mention a condom, just assume I'm using one. I don't know where my clients have been and, more to the point, I know where I have. OK. Back to it.

She looked up.

'I want you in me,' she said.

Once I had the condom, I gently pushed her back up.

'OK. Very happy to oblige,' I said, tearing the wrapper.

'It's OK,' she said. 'You don't need that.'

'Erm, yes we do,' I said, trying as best as I could not to start an argument.

'It's OK,' she said, pulling me towards her. Her dripping pussy was hard to resist, but some rules aren't worth breaking.

'Look. I don't mean to insist, but you don't know where I've been. And it's playing with fire.'

'It's OK,' she said, again. 'I'm on the pill.'

'My dear,' I said, 'I don't care if you're on all the pills in the world. We're using a condom or I'm going for an ice bath.'

She gave me a stern pout, but after a second seemed to soften. She took the condom and slid it down me, and I slowly moved forward taking us both down towards the sofa, before I eased my cock very slowly between her pussy lips. For a few minutes she seemed disappointed, almost disinterested. I leant back and pulled her up, so she was riding me, and in that position I shifted deep inside her, while playing with her clit. Even when she was coming, her eyes closed and teeth gritted hard, she seemed pissed off.

She stayed the night, and we had a second session, this time without disagreements about contraception. She left early, without much ceremony, and I assumed I wouldn't see her again.

But I was wrong. A week or so later, she called, and we agreed to meet again. I was in two minds, but figured that it was unlikely she would take the trouble to call and meet someone who she was still pissed off with.

We met in a different bar. She was perhaps even smarter and sexier than before. We sat in a booth and I bought drinks.

'Cesc,' she said, taking a sip. 'I wanted to see you again to apologise.'

'What for?' I said.

'The, you know. The condom thing.'

'Oh. Right. That's OK.'

'No. It's not. It was irresponsible. I don't know what came over me.'

I stifled a pun.

'It's OK. It's nothing. People say all sorts of strange things during, well, in intimate moments.'

'Yes. But it's not just that. I was trying to get you to get me pregnant.'

I coughed messily into my beer.

'What? Pregnant? Really?'

'Yes,' she said, with an embarrassed smile.

'Why me?'

'No offence meant, but it was nothing to do with you. Well, not really. I thought you'd be a good enough candidate. I don't know what came over me. It just happens sometimes. I just have an urge.'

'But aren't you worried that prostitution might be genetic?'

She sniggered. 'Cesc. What a silly thing to say.'

'Well ... And what about frequenting prostitutes? That could be too. Can you imagine the crises that kid would have? And it would put a terrible squeeze on the profit margin. I wouldn't want to have to compete with my own offspring.'

'Maybe. But I'm seeing someone about it, you know. I'm just glad it was with someone who's responsible. A lot of men would have just taken advantage of the situation.'

'Well, that's probably a bit unfair on us as a sex.'

She raised her eyebrows.

'Anyway. Can I make it up to you?' she said, with a look that was half expectant, half seductive. And she did,

133

too.

This time we went back to her place, a neat, modern flat near the river. She poured drinks and dimmed the lights. I sipped my whisky on the sofa while she disappeared into another room. She returned, with a shimmy that accentuated her lithe shape. Without music, she slowly stripped for me. In only her knickers and high heels, she clicked over the floor towards me and then knelt in front of me. She took a sip of whisky, and then, without swallowing, unzipped me and took me in her mouth. The whisky stung against my penis, but it aroused me more. I leant back, enjoying her technique again, while trying to hold myself back.

Then, she drew back, swallowed the whisky, and took a cube of ice in her mouth. The cold against the head of my cock sent shards of icy pleasure through my body. Meanwhile, I took a cube of my own. I sucked its edges off as she carried on her chilly blow job and then pushed her back. I reached down and slid the smooth ice into her pussy. She quivered with surprise and pleasure. Still sitting, I turned her round. I took another, smaller cube, and gently slid it into her, before quickly putting on a condom and lowering her buttocks until her pussy was on my cock. As I entered her, we both moaned with the intense sensation of cold and pleasure. She played with her clit while I pulled hard on her nipples, and soon she was coming noisily, her head back, her long ponytail flailing around in my face.

Then we went down onto all fours; her next orgasm was even noisier, as I slid deep in and out of her, a combination of her coming and the ice cubes gushing down her thighs. Soon I could no longer hold back, and her final orgasm coincided with me pulsating deep inside her.

'Does that make up for the other night?' she asked.

'I think you can worry too much about these things,' I said, rolling away from her. 'But yes, at least,' I said, fearing I might have pissed her off again. But the great thing about people who are sensitive about offending you is the lengths they'll go to make it up.

Being used as some sort of walking sperm bank didn't worry me so much that I stopped working for her, but it was clear that I was a stopgap until someone who was not just able but also willing to make some babies came along, and preferably wasn't a male prostitute. For a few weeks, we both got something that we wanted, although in her case not *the* thing. But I found out not long after she stopped calling me that she'd found an older guy and family life was the order of the day.

Chapter Twenty-eight

Julia and Z., like most of the clients who came to me because of the cards, did so because they were both very specific sorts of fantasists, who wanted a very specific sort of pleasure or service. I'm not sure whether it was anything to do with the cards themselves, or simply coincidence, but that tended to be the way. Friends of Celeste and passing trade came for more standard types of enjoyment, but the connoisseurs often came brandishing a business card.

I've told you about the girl with the strap-ons, right? Well the other, really quite strange fantasist was an elderly lady with a food sex fetish. I never quite identified how this particular interest of hers had developed, or really got much time to discuss it with her. And it was possibly the strangest assignment that I had.

The woman was an artist, living in a curious flat on the way towards the Heath. She'd made a lot of money buying and selling art in the Eighties, and had retired to muck about with paintings and entertain a series of gentlemen friends. I wasn't entirely sure what my role was going to be when she called up and invited me to visit. I'm not ageist, and I was perfectly ready to perform to the best of my abilities, regardless of an age gap of at least thirty years.

I wandered in to find a room that was part studio, part study and part bomb site. There were half-finished oil paintings in easels, piles of books on the rickety wooden floor and strange bits of experimental sculpture on makeshift plinths. Even stranger was that she offered me tea. I accepted.

'Now, I understand that you're a professional.'

'You understand correctly.' I struggled for a second for what to call her: Madam might well be a turn-off, while going straight to first-name terms seemed just rude.

'Please, call me Agnes,' she said. I nodded.

She continued. 'You see, I was thinking of just using one of my models for this. But you can't always guarantee discretion. And some of them might run a mile. I even used to have a chap who did this for me, you know, just for fun. But he's gone away now. So that's why I've got you here.'

'Of course. What is it you want?'

'Well I hope you don't think this is strange. I mean, really, it's very simple, you see. I'm going to eat off you. And then you're going to, you know, screw me.'

I nodded. 'I can do that. Believe me, it's not that strange,' I lied.

I noticed that there was a long, mahogany table, about a foot lower than a normal dining table.

'Up there?' I asked.

'Yes.'

I stripped, slowly, and then climbed up. I lay on my back, and she left the room. As I lay, the sheer oddness of it seemed to turn me on. By the time she was back, I had a prominent hard-on.

'Already?' she said, laughing to herself.

Luckily, I thought to myself, as she laid out a selection of cold meats, asparagus and tomatoes across my naked body, there was no soup course. With her lips and tongue, she carefully ate the first course, before disappearing again and reappearing with what smelt and looked like a pasta dish. She spread the food over my chest, my stomach and around my penis, which stuck out

137

of the dinner like an unexpected meat course. This time she used a knife and fork, twirling the pasta, running it against my nipples and groin. I was surprised to find myself turned on even more.

After the main course, she used a rough cloth to clean down her 'plate'. Then returned with what appeared to be a sticky cake. This was smeared on, rather than placed, and soon she was licking my stomach and groin, and then my balls and cock. I rose up in pleasure, pushing my cock into her mouth.

'Naughty. Tables don't move, you know,' she said, lifting her head away. 'But I think it's time for real dessert.'

She licked off the last of the cake before slipping out of her long house dress. She was naked underneath, and despite her age still firm bodied. I helped her up onto the table and then entered her from behind. She was excited and wet, and I was ready to enjoy myself. I leant back and closed my eyes, enjoying the sensation of sex combined with the sticky tightness of the remnants of her meal. It's my turn to eat, I thought to myself.

The food had clearly done its aphrodisiac duty, and soon she was coming in long, breathy shakes. I pushed the tip of my tongue to the roof on my mouth, tensed my cock inside her and then continued. Her second orgasm was bigger than the first, and her shaking almost had me come again. But I held off, and pulled out of her. I lay her back down, removed the condom and wanked over her naked body. She opened her mouth wide, and I spurted hot stripes of semen onto her tongue and down her throat, saving a few last drips to shoot onto her chin. Then I kissed her, savouring the taste of chocolate, saliva and my own orgasm.

'You're not the only gastronome here,' I said, as I

finished.

She sat up, licking her lips.

'Yes. I quite liked that. You can come here again,' she said.

Agnes became another regular, and every month she treated herself to a special meal. Like I said, I never quite worked out where this particular desire of hers came from. The evidence of her flat-cum-studio was of an eccentric, rather than a dedicated sexual adventurer like some of my other clients. I knew she was a gastronome – the menu changed for every session – and from the number of male nudes on the walls it was clear that she had a great appreciation of the male form. But unless my clients want to tell me, I don't start asking questions. I'm a call guy, not a private detective, and you can construct any pun you like out of that sentence.

Chapter Twenty-nine

As I said, as a call guy, a lot of my job is spent fulfilling the wildest fantasies that women can come up with. These include things you wouldn't want to and probably couldn't mention to a partner or your more conservative friends. The advantage in using me is that money buys silence and discretion. But not all the fantasies went quite to plan, at least not for me.

As well as seeing J., my first client, for our frequent sessions, we'd also exchange texts and emails using *The Joy of Cesc*'s own web page and email address – I've never been one to miss out on a technological advantage.

J. would suggest things to me, and occasionally we'd manage to come up with new things to do. She wasn't a demanding client, but she knew what she liked.

One day, via text, J. told me that she wanted to try Viagra. I called her back.

'Do we need it?' I said after a brief exchange.

'No, but I'd like to try.'

I was worried by the suggestion: it seemed like my professionalism was under question.

'But is there anything wrong with the sex at the moment?' I asked.

'No. But can you imagine what it would be like if it was better?'

I thought for a few seconds. She had a point.

'Can you get some?' I asked.

'A woman in my position? I certainly wouldn't be willing to risk my reputation buying dodgy pharmaceuticals.'

'Right,' I said. 'Well I'll have a word with a few

friends of mine, shall I?'

Curiously, that afternoon I had fifteen or more emails from various sources advertising garant33d m3d5, including v1agr@ and a series of other products they weren't permitted to spell correctly.

Instead, I phoned a couple of friends. Generally, they laughed at me, but Archie, my most cynical friend, seemed to take an interest.

'Cesc, my boy,' he said. 'Whatever does a fit young chap like you need that for?'

I should explain: Archie is the son of a publishing millionaire. He lives in his father's former bachelor pad over on the Heath, and makes a fairly unconvincing attempt to pretend he has to work for a living writing occasional pieces for magazines and teaching a class or two at his old university. We'd met via mutual friends from one college or another, and he seemed to enjoy having me around while he boozed and ranted.

Why had I asked him? Let's just say that Archie is a man familiar with chemical assistance. He must be the same age as me, but by his clothes, his accent and his frame, you wouldn't think he was a day younger than sixty.

'Well, it's complicated,' I said, wondering whether I should explain my new profession or not.

'Well, surely you can't have a problem?' he blustered.

'Don't ask personal questions, Archie. You know it's very insensitive.'

'Yeah, whatever, my boy. Whatever. Look, I think I know a man who can. But only if you tell me what's actually going on.'

I took a deep breath.

'OK. But not over the phone. Let's go for a drink.

Can you get the stuff first?'

'If you insist, my boy, if you insist.'

I met Archie in a pub near the Heath later that day. He had on parts of two three-piece suits that looked like they had been inherited at least twice, and he was on what looked like his third or fourth pint.

'Cesc, good to see you, let me let you get yourself a drink.'

'Thanks, Archie.' I ordered a pint and one more for him, and then sat down.

'Have you seen the girl at the bar?' asked Archie.

I had. She was a tall Slavic-looking girl …

'With the most amazing cleavage,' finished off Archie.

'I noticed,' I replied.

'We are attracted to it, naturally, you know,' explained Archie.

'What?' I said. He would often begin such flights of fancy, leaving me lost.

'It's because,' he continued, 'they look like bums.'

'What?'

'Cleavage. It takes us back to our animal days. I'm sure Freud said something about it.'

'Freud wrote about cleavage?'

'No, no. Cleavage looks like, well, arse cleavage. It reminds us of animalistic coitus.'

I looked at him blankly.

'Sex from behind, Cescy. And that's why we find it attractive.'

I thought about what Archie was saying for a second.

'Is that how you weaned yourself off men, Archie?' I said.

He spat his beer back into the glass.

'You bastard, Cesc. Now, shut up, and tell me, what's

all this about?'

'Archie, can you keep a secret?'

'No. But I might forget it. Certainly if I have a couple more of these.'

'OK. Well I'm … How can I put this? I'm fucking for money.'

'Fucking for money. I never realised you were, you know. A homo.'

'Archie, don't be prejudiced. And no one uses that word anyway. Besides, it's with women.'

'Christ! Women pay to have your obscene member inserted in them. Times must be a-changing.'

'Cheers, mate. I'll have you know I've got quite a distinguished client list already.'

'Well. I'm impressed. So what's up? Wearing you out, is it?'

'No. It's a client. She wants to try it.'

'Can women use it?'

'Archie, do you have any contact with the modern world at all?'

'I'm a historian. Get another round in will you, pal, I'm a bit strapped.'

'You're the heir to the biggest media fortune in London. How can you be strapped?'

'Don't bring my family into this. Now, do you want the stuff or not?'

I went to the bar and returned. Archie left a box of pills on the table.

'By the way, is this legal?' I asked.

'From my point of view, yes. This is my prescription. I just happen to have left it discarded on the table. I'll have you know I had to humiliate myself by feigning impotence to a private doctor. It didn't help that she was a stunner and I had the raging horn all the way through

143

the consultation.'

I pocketed the meds and handed him some cash under the table.

'I don't know why you're giving me money, Cesc,' he said.

'Let's just say I'm feeling generous,' I answered, playing along with the sham.

A couple of punters were eyeing us suspiciously, so we decided to leave. I said goodbye to Archie at the door of the pub and headed back to the flat.

I've never been a fan of medical aids, be they sexual or otherwise. I don't pop pills, and I'll normally soldier on through illness. As for sex aids, I've got nothing against vibrators, dildos, toys, whatever, but I'm reasonably convinced that unless you've got a serious problem, if it doesn't come up when necessary then it's probably a message of some sorts from somewhere, or quite possibly a good get-out clause. But J. was a good client and I'd never tried the stuff before, so I thought it would be at least worth a go.

I considered trying the stuff before the session, or asking Celeste if she'd be our guinea pig, but decided not to. That way, at least we'd enjoy the element of surprise, and I wouldn't have to put up with a chemically assisted and sexually frustrated Celeste scratching around the flat.

I saw J. at her place and we chatted amiably for a while before she mentioned the pills. I produced them and made up some story about where I'd got them. I suggested that we should just try a bit of a pill each, or a half, but J. was a hedonist who I'd discovered had been an enthusiastic member of the rave generation, and was not in the mood for half measures.

We took one of the little pills each, and I settled in to

giving J. a long massage while we waited for the effects to kick in. In her case, the results were more immediate.

'Mmm,' she said, as I ran my palms up her thighs. 'It's starting to tingle.'

'Funny. I can't feel anything yet.'

I continued with the massage, paying particular attention to her buttocks and the small of her back. She began to squirm slightly against the bed, her broad hips moving rhythmically as she took pleasure from my hands and the feeling of the soft sheets against her breasts and groin.

'It's definitely working,' she said. The thought of being inside her was getting me hard, regardless of the medication, so it was tricky to tell. But I had to admit a faint warming sensation. I ran my hands the length of her back, and then leant forward to kiss her thighs and work my mouth towards her pussy. As she lifted her hips to meet my tongue, I could see her arousal. Her lips and clit were incredibly sensitive, and she moaned with pleasure at the first touch of my tongue against her sex. I reached under her and cupped her breasts while savouring the juices of her excitement, pushing my tongue deep into her for several strokes and then licking hard up and down her clit as she rocked gently against her rhythm.

'I don't want to come yet, stop,' she said.

'Really?' I pulled back and gently slid a finger into her, then out and along to her quivering clitoris. Her nipples were now like bullets. She turned around off all fours and lay down, running her own hands down her body and along her thighs. I noticed that my cock was extremely erect, without her having even touched it. That wasn't a surprise in itself, but I hadn't really noticed it coming up. I flicked the shaft: it was solid.

'Fuck me hard, and don't stop,' she said, running her

fingers down either side of the edges of her pussy. I slipped on a condom and entered her. Her legs spread further to take me deeper inside, and I worked myself between her thighs so I was right inside her with my groin pressed against her throbbing clit. In a sort of press-up position I was able to thrust hard inside her while rubbing against her. Her arousal was amazing: her first orgasm was the loudest, most violent she'd had with me, only to be topped by a second one, her legs wrapped around my thighs, her nails embedded into my back, screaming at me for more. I came myself, a deep, powerful orgasm that seemed to stem from the very roots of my cock and balls and draw force from every thrust. As we lay, sweaty and shaking, I noticed that my erection hadn't gone down. J. noticed too.

'Go on then. Why waste an opportunity,' she said. I pulled out and turned her round. Despite coming, my dick was even harder than before; J.'s pussy was wet with her own excitement, and still as sensitive as when I'd first licked her. I entered her, slowly at first, but with increasing speed and strength. The shouts of her coming made me think I might have hurt her, but soon I could make out 'More' and 'Harder' amongst the cries. By the time I'd come again, I was pumping with a rhythm that made my heart pound and which I feared for a moment might do one of us some damage. My cock was as hard as a dildo and showed no signs of going down.

It was my fitness that let me down eventually. After that second, breathless orgasm, I collapsed to the side, J. lying panting beside me. She looked down.

'Still hard,' she said.

'What about you?' I said.

'It feels nice.'

We both needed a breather before starting up again.

Feeling lazy after my efforts, I had her ride me. The sight of her large breasts and of her squeezing and tweaking them turned me on even more. I held her hips and helped her bounce to another orgasm on my rigid dick.

'It's so good,' she shouted, shifting a hand down to stroke her clitoris to another, quick but noisy climax. Her rocking orgasm was enough to finish me off, and I could feel the last, acidic juices of my coming in the end of the condom. I winced, mixing the intense pleasure of our mutual climaxes with a definite sense of possibly having overdone it.

As we lay side by side, J. smoking and I trying to get my breath back, I noticed that my erection hadn't gone down.

'Do you think that's right?' I asked her.

'How long have we been at it for?' she asked.

I looked at the clock.

'Quite a while. And I've come three times.'

'Well let's see if one more makes a difference, shall we?'

She moved slowly down the bed, kissing my stomach and my thighs. Soon, my balls were in her mouth, being gently sucked and kissed while she softly ran her fingers up the shaft. Then she ran her tongue up the length, lightly stroking the rim and the tip. Her blow jobs were excellent and well practised, and she could deep-throat me without problems. I savoured the sensation of her lips running down my length, the suction in her mouth and the rhythmic contact of my head against the back of her mouth. She had another trick, which was to hum very lightly, turning her whole mouth into a vibrating chamber for my penis.

As my excitement grew I put my hands to her hair,

147

holding it away from her face while dictating the speed of her strokes. She used one hand to stroke my chest and another to tease my balls and stroked around my buttocks, and soon I was coming in arching thrusts, pumping what was left of my semen into the back of her throat. She swallowed without so much as blinking, staring me hard in the eye all through my orgasm.

J. rolled away, seemingly exhausted. But my erection still hadn't gone down.

I went and showered, first using the hot to clean myself and then turning the dial across to cold. Everything in my body tensed up with the shock of the icy water. Everything, that is, except my erection, which remained standing proud.

As I towelled myself off, J. looked at me admiringly.

'It's a pity you have to go,' she said. 'We could put that to some more use.'

'You're insatiable,' I said, landing a brief kiss on her cheek.

'That's why you're still in work,' she said. She replaced me in the shower while I dressed, picked up the envelope with my pay and left. By now, my cock was starting to feel uncomfortable. It's one thing having a raging hard-on stuck inside a sexy client, it's another having one stuck inside your jeans, stuck inside a taxi.

Back at the flat, I asked Celeste. She was lounging around in a dressing gown and an old, long T-shirt, recovering from a day-and-a-half-long hangover.

'Have you ever taken, you know, medical assistance? Pills?' I said.

'No. I don't think girls can take it.'

'Apparently they can. And with quite spectacular effects.'

I realised that she was looking at me. Or rather,

checking me out.

'What's up?' I said.

'Well, I'm hardly looking my best, so I'm very flattered.'

'What are you talking about?'

She nodded towards my groin. My erection was clearly visible, even through my jeans.

'Thanks, but you're not putting that anywhere near me. I know where you've been.'

'No offence, Cel, but it's nothing to do with you.'

Her eyes widened as revelation dawned.

'Ohh. You've taken it. Have you got a date? Feeling a bit nervous? Poor you.'

'I've *had* a date.'

Her face fell. 'Oh. Really poor you. Won't it go down?'

'No.'

'How many times have you, you know …'

'Several. I may have lost count.'

'And when did you start?'

'Ages ago.'

She thought for a moment, pulling a series of concerned faces that I imagined she'd learnt from medical dramas.

'Maybe you should see a doctor?'

'It's a bit hard to explain, isn't it? I'm a gigolo, and I've sourced a load of semi-legal sex pills, shagged for about five hours and can't get my erection to go down.'

Celeste stifled a laugh.

'It does sound a bit funny, yes.'

'Funny is not the word,' I said, almost bitterly.

The next morning, once I'd realised that my severe case of morning glory was fast becoming mid-morning and lunchtime glory, I called my doctor. One of the perks of the trade was that I could justify private medicine to myself, particularly as I liked to get myself checked regularly for any nasties that, despite sensible precautions, I could pick up along the way.

I went to a slick little clinic in Hampstead, and they were quite used to my more than occasional presence and my concern for matters related to sexual health. I think my regular doctor, a sexy little Japanese medic, not long out of training, who wore excessively short skirts and those glasses on a cord that suggest sweaty and perverse sex, had probably guessed something of my profession.

'So, Mr Aleixandre, what can I do for you today?' she asked with a suggestion of a smile.

'You can keep a secret, right?'

'I'm a doctor. It's the Hippocratic oath.'

'Right. So that means this goes no further?'

'Of course.'

'Basically, I sourced some dodgy meds from a friend, took some, had lots of sex and now my erection won't go down.'

'Right.'

'Do you want to take a look?'

'Yes, I think I'd better. Go behind the screen and strip from the waist.'

I did as requested, and sat on the bed. The doctor came in. I realised that I might well have had an erection just thinking about her, but it was hard to differentiate with the effects of the drugs.

'Well, it's definitely an erection,' she said. 'How long has it been up for?'

I was impressed at her matter-of-fact questions. But I guess that as sexy as she was, first and foremost she was just another professional.

150

'A day or so.'

'Right. Well I'm just going to have a closer look, to make sure there's no damage.'

Luckily, I don't have a rubber glove fetish, otherwise I might well have come over her there and then. She gently held and examined my penis.

'There doesn't appear to be any major damage.'

Anyone who walked in would have assumed I was getting sucked off. I tried to banish the thought immediately from my mind.

'There's some chafing. Have you been having a lot of sex?'

'Well, I don't think so.'

She looked at me.

I gave in under her stare.

'At least every day,' I admitted.

'And since you took the pill?'

'Pretty much constantly.'

'Right,' she said, with a slightly disapproving shake of the head. 'Well I think you should go easy for a few days, and if nothing changes, come back. You can get dressed now,' she added, stepping back out through the curtain, leaving me with my hard-on and a distinct sense of frustration. If only life were like porno movies, I thought, ruefully watching her leave me.

A good patient, I did as she asked, even cancelling one of my regulars – I told her I had conjunctivitis, as a permanent erection is no decent excuse to cancel work as a male prostitute. After several cold showers and a day watching knitting programmes and farming digests on digital TV, finally, the fellow went down. It was both a relief and a disappointment to see my member at its normal size and angle. But I'd learnt my lesson: chemical assistance should only be for those who really need it.

Chapter Thirty

It didn't take too long for me to be back at work properly, although I made it clear that from then on the only assistance we were using required batteries.

But it wasn't the only out-of-the-ordinary request that I got in my early months as a call guy. I realised that women often called not necessarily because what they were asking was in some way scandalous, perverse or dangerous, or because they were embarrassed about wanting or needing a particular form of pleasure, but because they didn't want anyone to think that they were silly.

The best example came a few weeks after my incident with the erection that wouldn't go down. I got a call from a landline, a number in London. The lead-in was pretty much as expected.

'Is that the Joy of Cesc?'

'Yes, Cesc speaking.'

'Oh, it's a name, I see. Erm, you, you have sex for money, right?'

'Right.'

'Do you do costumes?'

The answer, of course, was yes. At length, she explained what she wanted, and when I hesitated for a second, she began a detailed explanation of the circumstances that had led her to want to recreate this particular fantasy situation.

With the time and place decided, I set about sourcing my outfit. I tried a fancy dress shop, which simply didn't look realistic enough. I phoned a couple of friends with no success. Eventually, I remembered an old costume supplier I'd visited once when acting in a play as a student, back in the days when I was set on an acting career, rather than a fucking career.

I found what I was looking for: an outfit that was convincing, fitted and had a very slight air of the comic about it. I thanked the elderly luvvie who manned the shop and headed home with the kit.

At the flat Celeste spent almost an hour taking the piss out of my costume, how I looked in the costume and the series of increasingly ridiculous puns that could be made about the role I was playing, mostly jokes about helmets and hoses. She also pointed out that I was bordering on turning into a cheesy stripper-gram, which I was forced to accept, with the exception that as well as getting naked I was also going to give the client the screw of a lifetime. Celeste shrugged, and left me to it.

I packed my kit into a large holdall and called a taxi. The address was across the river, a three-floor town house in a posh cul-de-sac close to Blackheath. I buzzed and went in through the ground floor entrance. As I'd been instructed, there was a little cloakroom, where I changed into my kit. Then I went through to the walled garden, where my client had been good enough to leave a long ladder.

I waited, and soon I heard screams from an open upstairs window. Stepping into character, I propped the ladder up, and began my climb. As I climbed, I saw smoke coming out, and as I poked my head up, saw a woman in her thirties flapping around a flaming bin while a smoke alarm went off.

I pulled myself in through the window and announced my arrival.

'It's OK, madam, I'm here now.' I used a little fire extinguisher attached to the wall to put out the flames, and as the smoke filled the room, I swept her up into my arms. There was, I'll admit, something of the ridiculous about the scene, but as I carried her to the window, she was kissing me passionately, running her hands through my hair and almost dislodging my helmet.

She was, as you've no doubt guessed, a fireman fetishist. As she'd explained on the phone, she had been rescued from a burning house as a young teenager, and had spent years fantasising about tall, dark heroes in yellow rubber trousers. She'd even had a fireman boyfriend, but had found that his professionalism would not allow him to play the fantasy games that she wanted. He refused, I later found out, to either allow her to attend emergencies or to fake them for her. Now that she was a wealthy professional, she could recreate the scenes just as she desired.

I spun her around onto my back where she gripped tightly. The step out of the window was tricky, but I'd been practising at home, and soon we were down in the garden. The smoke had ceased billowing from the window, but we were both sweaty and sooty. We tumbled onto the grass as she kissed me and tore open my jacket. She was a pretty, brown-haired thirty-something, and as I slipped off her dress I noticed a large scar across her shoulder and arm: a burn, I imagined.

'My hero,' she said, drawing me towards her. I hitched up her dress, pulled down her knickers and began to kiss and tongue her sex. I found the fireman's helmet rather awkward, but she refused to let me remove it. She hadn't come when she pulled me up and asked for me to enter her. I pushed her dress over her head, revealing small but well-formed breasts. I sucked her nipples while teasing her clitoris with my fingers, as she greedily tore open my fly. Soon I was in her, my jacket torn open and her buttocks grinding into the wet turf.

As her breathing quickened and the first signs of orgasm became clear, I leant back and drew her up. She sat in my lap, wrapped up in my arms, and rocked on my thighs, flinging her head back and stroking her breasts and clit. She came quietly but energetically, falling back with relief as her climax ran through her body.

'Come on me,' she said, falling back on the turf.

I wriggled out from under her and removed the condom. I used one hand to stimulate her sex, and the other to wank myself off, while she stroked my balls and her nipples. Her second climax coincided with the height of my arousal, and as she was shaking with pleasure, I fired a hot stream of cum onto her tits and neck. The last few drops she took in her mouth, enthusiastically sucking in what was left.

A few minutes later, as we lay, satisfied and messy, she turned to me.

'You saved my life,' she said.

'Just doing my job,' I replied.

Chapter Thirty-one

Along with the fantasies and scenarios, much of my work as a call guy is related to that very specialised science of female pleasure: giving head.

There is a big difference between giving head to a man and giving it to a woman. Put simply, it's almost impossible to give a bad blow job. Just by existing, a blow job is good. Some women are better than others, but there is no such thing as worse.

But men who don't know what to do, who try and fail, I'm told, can be as annoying and frustrating as men who refuse to go anywhere near it.

A lot of my clients come to me asking very specifically for good head. On the one hand, cunnilingus can be gauged simply by result: if the girl in question comes to a screaming climax, then it's good stuff. But there are different types of good, and different things that women want to get out of a good tongue-lashing.

Sophie, for example, the young anorgasmic fiancée, had come to me, pretty much, looking for someone who knew how to give good head. She'd never had an orgasm just through sex. She'd told me that her fiancé would happily go down on her, but never had the patience to keep at it, and always stopped before she'd come so that he could take his own pleasure. Poor schmuck probably didn't even know he was doing anything wrong.

Sophie needed time and patience. She was surprisingly self-conscious, and once even told me, after one of our sessions, that she was worried about looking ugly when she came. I almost laughed – she was cute and petite all the time, and when she came, with enthusiastic, noisy gasps, I found it irresistibly exciting. But it took her a long time to relax. With her I'd always make sure she got a long massage, or we showered together, or sometimes we'd just sit and chat, to calm her nerves and to get her used to me.

In bed, I spent a lot of time pleasuring her with my mouth and tongue. She took a long time to come, and often I would deliberately prolong the pleasure, moving away from her clit to tease her lips or to enter her with my tongue. As I returned to her clit, she grasped my hair and moaned instructions to me. I tended to ignore these so that I could enjoy spending more time tasting her arousal. Even the loud gasps as she climaxed had something cute about them.

Other girls had different desires. J., for example, liked hard and insistent stimulation, and seemed to treat my tongue as a human vibrator. Her orgasms were energetic and full of action, and as I savoured her juices, I often risked a knee in the head or a foot in the stomach. Whereas with Sophie, I'd vary the rhythm to manipulate her pleasure, to tease out her climaxes, J. liked me to start quick and hard, to concentrate on her clit, and to work to a swift conclusion.

There were various options to consider: pressure, speed, rhythm and position. Some women required just the lightest of touches while others needed harder contact. Raven liked rapid movements, whereas V., Virginia, preferred feather-light touches – she argued that there was a certain subtlety that the tongue could achieve and her sex toys could not.

As for rhythm, when I'd gone down on Raven, it seemed that steadily speeding up gave the best results, although the same technique hadn't been so successful with Sophie. And with Sophie I liked to vary the object of my attentions, whereas my client from the gym preferred her clitoris to be the sole beneficiary of my efforts.

There were other little tricks that my clients liked. V., who was something of an intellectual, after all, liked me to tongue letters on her, and spell words. She would guess, and praise or question my technique. The mental effort, as well as the delayed and tantalising sensation as I spelt things out over her sex, seemed to prolong her pleasure and hold off her eventual climax. J. liked me to hum as I gave her cunnilingus, making my tongue and lips vibrate over her.

I've talked a lot about Sophie, and in a way that's because, as well as my most faithful client for oral sex, she was also quickly becoming my biggest problem. Firstly, as much as I enjoyed the sensation of my tongue against her neatly waxed pubis, I was always slightly concerned that her fiancé might return unexpectedly and kill me in a fit of jealous rage. I'd seen pictures: he was a big guy, and he practised martial arts. I was convinced he'd be able to tear my head off before I'd even realised he'd arrived.

Secondly, I realised I was getting drawn into her life in a non-professional way. We chatted, I told her things about myself, and we laughed a lot. She showed me new outfits and even sexy underwear that she'd bought, presumably to encourage her man to do his job in the sack properly.

In many ways she was perfect: petite, cute, funny and desperate for sex with me. Before I'd become a professional, the last girl I'd had a serious relationship with was a lot like her, both physically and as a person, although of course without the track record of intense sexual frustration and the potentially murderous partner.

But in other ways, Sophie was totally and utterly wrong: frequenter of male prostitutes, engaged to be married and with a history of being anorgasmic. And I realised that the more involved I got with her, the greater was the danger of me becoming unprofessional. I knew that I couldn't get into the habit of offering freebies, as much as I wanted to be with her. If my other Jennies found out that I was giving it away for nothing, I'd be ditched quicker than a used condom.

But there was no way that a nice girl like Sophie was going to end up living happily ever after with a guy she could pick up in a phonebook or from a card on the board in sex shops. Apart from the little problem with sex, she was perfectly happy with her fiancé. He was by all accounts a good guy, with a successful job and a respectable family who got on perfectly with hers.

I also got the impression that she was using me as a way to cure what she saw as a psychological problem, and once she'd become used to coming with me, she'd be able to translate that to other men, specifically the man she wanted to marry. Then, I imagined, regardless of what I felt or did, I was likely to have my unwritten contract permanently terminated.

My job was also a problem: she kept activities with me very much a secret, unlike, for example, Raven and her friend, who pretty much swapped notes, and J., who devoted quite a lot of effort to touting me to her friends. I just couldn't imagine Sophie being particularly happy in a proper relationship with a man whose job was boning other women. How do you explain that at a family dinner? Sorry, Cesc's got to pop out for the afternoon, he's got a client who needs to be bound, gagged and insulted. I'd have to be some sort of male Roxanne, putting out my red light for her. I doubted that she'd ask.

The question of seeing her outside of work was also a problem. Our paths crossed a few times – once in a pub, once in the queue at Waitrose. But she ignored me totally, and I had to respect that from a professional point of view.

Eventually, a month or so later, after a session with her in which, deep in a passionate fuck, I'd thought of telling her how I felt, circumstances intervened.

'Cesc, I'm sorry to let you down, but I can't carry on seeing you.'

I smiled and held my face in a pleasant mask.

'OK. Can I ask how come?'

'I'm getting married.'

'I thought you were engaged already.'

'No. We're actually getting married, date and everything.'

She told me the rest, briefly and almost coldly. Her long engagement was to turn into a proper marriage, and her fiancé, now properly set to be her husband, had decided that he spent far too long away from home and that they needed a bigger place, somewhere out of the smoke. That was our last session. I found out later that she'd moved out of the city. I texted her once, ready to pretend it was a mistake. The number came up as unregistered. Once I found myself walking past her old flat. There was a sold sign outside. Like that, she was gone.

Sophie was a lesson to me. I realised that I needed to control my feelings, and that in some way, if a girl was really sexy, I needed to be even more careful.

Chapter Thirty-two

I didn't mope over Sophie, mostly because I was too busy. I was pleasantly surprised that my escort work also took off. In part, this was less satisfying, as it didn't always end in sex. But it was also relatively easy money – all I had to do was dress appropriately (although never too showily, as it didn't do to outdo the client), smile lots and avoid mentioning what I really did for a living.

J. even took me to a few dos, including weddings and business functions. I've never been one to turn down free booze and food, and there was even the possibility for some shenanigans with other wedding guests if my client let me off the hook. J. was very good like that, and on one occasion even set me up with a bridesmaid, a distant cousin of hers, at a do she took me to.

J. had hired me at the last minute after a fellow consultant from her partnership had pulled out, claiming work commitments. She was annoyed with him, and I'm not sure whether hiring me for the event was some way of getting back at someone. I'm not quite sure who. I knew she didn't like weddings, and in conversations I also got the impression that she didn't like much of her own family.

I met her in a bar close by, and we took a taxi. I knew the venue from a bar job I'd done a few years before. The taxi was greeted by a top-hatted doorman and we joined a throng of guests on the thick carpet on the foyer.

The wedding was a swanky do at a private club in central London, colour coordinated, elegant and very expensive. I couldn't work out whether they'd chosen the ushers' outfits to match the venue, or had the decor changed. Either way, it was thoroughly thought out. We followed a flower-lined route through the foyer and into a modern, sleek hall where the ceremony was to take place. Subtle ambient music was playing in background, but there was also a pianist preparing in the corner. J. greeted a few friends and relatives, introduced me to these people as Jake, a friend, and I smiled and gave brief but friendly answers to those sort of polite questions you get asked by people you'll never meet again.

In the hall I surveyed the scene, in part checking for any familiar faces that might cause an identity crisis. I could rely on my Jennies for discretion – and quite a few knew J., anyway. It was a good-looking wedding – the couple were young, her parents were wealthy and they had drawn a well-dressed gang of society London. I commented on the gathering to J. and she nodded.

'You're always on the prowl, Cesc.'

'Jake. The name is Jake,' I said, maintaining my smile and standing as the bride entered.

'Wow,' I said, seeing her. 'She's a stunner.'

'You should see her sister,' J. replied.

I looked past the bride, a slim, fine-boned beauty wearing a long, cream, silk gown that fell beautifully over her shoulders and collarbone, and whose light brown hair had been swept up into an artistic swirl. Behind her, however, was her younger sister, wearing a shorter, dark version of the same dress, and who instead of the saintly look of her sister had the voluptuous figure, jet-black bobbed hair and cheeky look in her eyes of a sexy little mischief-maker.

'I see her. I see her. If I didn't know you, I'd think you wanted me to misbehave.'

J. turned to me and raised her eyebrows. 'I'm not

saying that. You might want to, but I certainly …'

I missed the last couple of words as the bridal march rose to a crescendo.

The ceremony struck the right balance between emotion and elegance, and for the first time that I could remember I enjoyed a wedding ceremony. The bridesmaids and the ushers were all uniformly perfect, and even the little kids looked like they'd been grafted in from a children's wear catalogue. I tried to work out which bridesmaid went with which usher. As we filed out, I turned to J. and whispered the question to her.

'The sister is single, if that's what you're asking.'

'That's not what I'm asking. I'm just curious, you know.'

We were interrupted by a silent waiter, moving as if on rollers, offering champagne and cocktails of varying shades. I took a glass of champers; J. chose a glass of pink. I sipped mine, while J. chugged hers and reached for another from a different waiter travelling in the opposite direction. She also found a tray of canapés and handed me some hors d'oeuvres.

'Here. Make sure you're well fed.'

She slid off into a crowd, leaving me holding a drink and what looked like a quail's egg in a tiny basket of grass. As I wondered whether I could leave it in a vase, I turned to face the sister of the bride.

'Hi. I'm Jackie,' she said.

'Funny coincidence. I'm Jake.'

'I'm sure we've met somewhere before,' she said, turning her head on one side and giving me a look that could have spelt either sex or expulsion.

'I'm sure I'd have remembered you,' I answered. 'Excellent reading, by the way. Will you be giving a speech?' I asked.

163

'Of course,' she answered with a smile.

'I look forward to it. Will you excuse me? Sorry to be rude, but I think my date needs me.'

I left her half hanging and moved through the crowd. J. had cast me a look as an elderly bore, who looked like he'd had a reception's worth of booze before the ceremony, was leering down her top. I linked arms with her and sped her away.

'Are you up to something?' I asked.

'No,' she replied, all innocence. 'But I can look after myself, you know.'

I sipped some more of my champagne and then after gravitating in and out of a few more conversations with strangers I found myself guided towards dinner.

It was another polished affair – white linen, coordinated table dressings and fancy favours for the lady guests. Even the speeches were passable; the drunken bore turned out to be the father of the bride, and he'd clearly tried rather too hard to steady his nerves. The sexy sister told some borderline jokes and had every man in the place hanging on her every word, and the best man kept his efforts mercifully short.

I soon realised, once we finished coffee and I was able to circulate amongst the guests, that I was a lot soberer that almost everyone around me, and that there was an air of palpable sexual tension. Much of it seemed to centre on the sister of the bride, who was flirting viciously, often with men who were clearly on the arm of another woman or even a wife.

The pianist had been stood down, and the first dance came and went before a few of the more, let's say, lubricated, couples began twirling dangerously on the floor. J. had disappeared and was chatting to a few of the people I'd seen her greet on our arrival, trying to avoid being dragged towards the dance floor. Meanwhile I rotated in and out of a series of friendly exchanges with people I'd never met, only forgetting on a couple of occasions my assumed name and the precise details of the identity I was meant to assume.

I've never, I must say, liked weddings very much: I split up with a girlfriend I was very fond of at one, and was punched at another. It was a case of mistaken identity, I should add. A Spanish guest had pinched someone's girlfriend's arse, and the offended boyfriend was ignorant enough to strike out at the first faintly foreign-looking person nearby, specifically me.

Yes, weddings do strange things to people. But, as I watched the beautiful, flirting crowds, I realised that the effects might not be solely negative. I caught a glimpse of a couple heading off furtively towards the upstairs rooms, and realised that the elegance of the venue, the attractiveness of the guests and the quantity of champagne seemed to be making everyone a little bit, well, randy.

As I observed the scene, I felt a chin on my shoulder. It was J.

'Cesc, I'm going to go in a while.'

'Really. Oh, why? Aren't you enjoying yourself?'

'No, I am. But I'm off to go and enjoy myself somewhere else. I hope you don't mind.'

For a moment, I was offended. J. had pulled when out with me. She made the merest of gestures towards the door, where a tall, well-built man in a kilt appeared to be waiting for something.

'I used to be a friend of his wife,' she said.

I realised that I was caught in a complicated web of family, friendships and age-old grudges.

'But don't worry,' continued J. 'The floor is yours.'

I realised she wasn't looking at me, but rather had somehow indicated to the sister of the bride that she should keep me company. Jackie politely but briskly abandoned the circle of admirers and cut through the crowds towards us.

'Jackie, you'll look after Jake, won't you?' purred J.

'Of course. Jake, do you dance?'

'Brilliantly,' I answered. The women smiled, and J. disappeared, smirking slightly. I offered Jackie my hand and led her, without a word, towards the dance floor.

I wasn't lying about the dancing, by the way, and you should remember that it's a difficult lie to keep up for long in any situation where there is music, a suitable space and a dance partner nearby. There was always music in my house when I was a youngster, and for reasons too complex to go into, I even did dance classes at school. When I was a student, thinking about acting, I imagined that musicals would be a lucrative career, so kept at the practice. As an escort, the ability to keep off your partner's toes and not do an impression of a drunken dad is very useful. And, of course, I've always loved a good boogie.

Jackie was an enthusiastic, if rather showy, dancer. I suspect that she was used to being the centre of attention on any dance floor – she had long, fit legs, and a body that suggested fun in bed, as well as hair she could shake all over only for it to return perfectly into style.

The DJ spun a tasteful selection of sixties and seventies classics and the occasional rarity. Around us, variations on popular dances such as of the 'vertical shag', the 'broken ankle' and the 'coughing fit' were getting a good shakedown. I held Jackie's waist and ran her through a few twirls, nothing too spectacular. Then from the booth emerged the strains of some Latin numbers. I drew her closer to me and executed some slightly more demanding moves, all of which gave an excuse for plenty of body contact, deep stares and breathy clinches. As one song drew to a close, I spun her in along the length of my arm, stopping her with our lips almost touching, and then whirled her back out. She kicked her heel down on the final note and hurled an arm into the air. Out of the bubble of the dance, I noticed that around us people were clapping.

I decided that I was in danger of becoming indiscreet, and the DJ was good enough to slow the tempo down. I pulled Jackie in towards me and we danced in a close clinch. Her heart was beating fast against my chest, and I noticed her quickened breathing and dilated pupils. She was clearly having a whale of a time. As we danced, I felt her nuzzling into my neck.

'You're an excellent dancer, you know.'

'Thanks. You're quite a mover yourself.'

'Men never know how to dance properly. Where did you learn?'

'I'm kind of from Argentina. I think it just comes naturally.'

'Really? Quite the mystery man.'

'There's no mystery about me.'

'Sure about that? Come on, let's go outside.'

She led me by the hand through the admiring crowd, and outside produced a packet of cigarettes from a sparkly clutch bag I hadn't seen with her inside.

'Smoke?'

'No, thanks,' I answered.

She looked at me with an analytical gaze. I got the impression she was trying to work something out about me. In the meantime, I could admire her figure, shown off by the little dress, and accentuated by her

167

spectacularly high heels.

'What's going on with you and …?'

'We're friends,' I interrupted. 'I don't think she likes coming to weddings on her own.'

'Who does?' she answered, her response half muzzled by her cigarette. Underneath the brash confidence, there was a note of vulnerability. I realised that her ability to impress was only matched by her need to do so. Out in the cold, she looked younger.

'Here, have my jacket. You must be cold.'

'A gentleman as well,' she said with a smile. I cast my suit coat around her shoulders. As I did, she threw her cigarette to one side and put her hands lightly to my face.

'Are you as perfect in bed, Mr Jake?' she said.

'I can be,' I said, as she kissed me, passionately, almost tumbling off her shoes.

'I have a room upstairs, room 15. I'll be there. I'm yours if you want me,' she said, leaving me on the pavement with a peck on the cheek as a reminder.

Leaning against the wall, I thought for a brief moment: I was probably stepping into some sort of complicated family saga. But I'd also be getting into bed with a stunner while being paid to date another woman. And, it might also get me over my dislike of weddings. After a break-up and a broken tooth, I felt they owed me something.

I gave her a few minutes while I watched tourists and drunken out-of-towners roaming the streets of the city. Back inside, the lift to the rooms was off a side corridor – a discreet arrangement that meant that no one had to make their post-wedding activities too obvious. I wondered whether J. might also be upstairs with her new-found Scottish gentleman.

I took the lift up a floor and walked along the plush corridor to her room. I knocked, once, and the door swung open. Inside, the room was more of a suite – a large bed along one side, a coffee table and chairs to the other, floor-to-ceiling sliding doors opening on to a balcony with views of the river and, in front of it, a long chaise longue on which Jackie was lounging like the most attractive and expensive piece of furniture in the whole place.

She spun round, showing off her long legs and leaning back against the chair.

'We haven't got long. They'll be expecting me back down there for the departure.'

'I can take as long or as short as you like,' I said.

'You are a tempter,' she said. As she crossed her legs I noticed that she had no knickers on.

I walked over and sat next to her, kissing her neck, by her ear, and then her sensual mouth as she twined her slim arms around my neck. She had a great body for sex: long limbs and generous breasts, and clearly gifted with athletic prowess. I lifted her up in my arms and carried her to the bed, half stumbling as I put her down. I found myself on top of her, the two of us bouncing on the thick mattress. She unbuttoned my shirt as we kissed, while I unzipped her dress and began to play with her nipples. She had no bra either, and soon she was naked except for her shoes. I kissed her breasts and toned stomach, and soon I was tasting her sex. Her pussy was neatly trimmed, slightly darker than her hair, and was wet with arousal. She stayed strangely silent as I teased and licked with my tongue, but I could tell from the pressure of her hands on my head, nails almost digging into my scalp, that she loved it. As I increased the strength of my tongue strokes, she kicked her legs in the air, gritting her teeth, as the first waves of orgasm flooded over her. She came very quickly, but the sensation was clearly no less intense. Her shaking almost threw me off, and I found my face pressed hard against her smooth groin.

As the quivering died down, I leant back and unzipped my fly. She scrabbled on to all fours, hitching my trousers down my ankles to allow better access to my cock. She sucked enthusiastically, if hurriedly, concentrating more on the end result than on the pleasure itself. But for me, the beautiful curves of her back and the cleft of her arse turned me on even more, and I stroked her silken hair and enjoyed.

Stopping myself coming, I realised there was a chance to do something I'd never done before.

'It's a great view you've got here,' I said to her.

She looked up, my penis still in her hand, slightly confused.

'What?' she said, shaking her hair away from her face.

'Come on,' I said, shifting away from her and taking her hand. I helped her off the bed and led her, still in her fuck-me heels, towards the balcony. Opening the door let in a gust of cold air, and as I guided her to the rail her tits and nipples went taut with the chill. I rolled on a condom and pushed her legs apart. She arched her back and shook her head as I slid my cock into her. She grasped the rail tight while I began to fuck her from behind. The view was marvellous – her form against the black of the night, the lights of the city and the stars above. I leant back and concentrated on the pleasure of her pussy against me, a finger stroking her clitoris from behind as I did.

On the balcony her policy of silence ceased. She gasped and moaned as I stroked and screwed her towards her second coming.

'Yes, come on, more. Don't stop,' she shouted at me and at the city. There was no danger of me stopping. I wondered whether we could be heard from the street below, and in a way hoped that we could be. We came together, her rapid shakes and clenches sending bolts of pleasure up my shaft as I ejaculated, deep inside her. I held her tight from behind until we had both finished our final shudders, and then we collapsed back inside the room.

Lying on the bed, still sexy and naked but for the shoes, she turned to me.

'I have to be downstairs. Can you see a pair of knickers anywhere?'

'I didn't think you had any on.'

'That was just for you, Jake. Or should I say, Chesc.'

'It's Cesc. And how do you know?'

'Let's just say that my present was better than anything my sister's getting.'

In a flash, she was dressed and on her way out. I took one last admiring look at her as she left through the door.

Present? I thought to myself. What on earth was she talking about? And how did she know my real name?

171

Chapter Thirty-three

Later, things started to fall into place. I don't think that Jackie was really meant to mention it to me, so in a way, I found out about the presents only by accident. Unable to resist, I asked J. about it at our next session.

'Well she's a silly girl for mentioning it,' she said with a shake of the head. 'You don't mind, do you? In a way you should be flattered.'

'What's the story, though?' I said.

J., it happened, had decided that I was an excellent present to give to friends, starting with Jackie, an old friend of the family about whom she felt rather protective. I wasn't quite sure what Jackie had done to deserve me as a gift, but J. had told her about me and offered, well, a unique way to mark her big sister's wedding day.

Reading between the lines, I got the impression that Jackie was feeling rather down about the whole affair, having split up with a boyfriend in the run-up to the wedding. That sort of explained her changing attitudes during our session – starting quiet and reserved, and then getting more enthusiastic as we went on. And that was also why she'd left me so quickly – there was no danger of her mistaking me for a possible relationship, and J. had been clear about the set-up. I was a hired fuck, a quick and decadent release, and that was that.

'You're not annoyed, are you?' J. asked.

'No. Of course not. I enjoyed myself. But you can tell me, you know, if you're going to set this sort of thing up.'

'Ah. You see that was part of the attraction. I knew I

could trust you. In fact, I heard you.'

'You weren't downstairs, were you?' I asked, remembering the arousing image of Jackie's perfect naked body leaning over the railings into the cold night.

'No. I was in room 17. It quite turned me on.'

'In that case, maybe I should charge double,' I joked.

So, just like that, I had become a very trendy and decadent gift that girls could bestow on their friends. It was quite simple, and seldom as elaborate as the set-up with J. and Jackie. The woman either got tipped the wink by her friend, or got a card in a little envelope. Meanwhile, I got a number and a cheque. Other than that, it tended to work much along the lines of a normal date, except that the payment came from a different source.

I wondered how the women felt, but then realised that it takes a good friend to tell you that what you really need is a damn good shag. It could also be, I came to realise, a very modern and classy alternative to the stripper on a hen night. I have become, apparently, the most decadent and trendy gift that can be given on such an occasion.

Rather than being forced into ridiculous fancy dress, made to down sickly drinks until you puke and then being mock humiliated by a muscle-bound exhibitionist, far more pleasant to spend a very decadent and discreet evening with a man who is trained for and dedicated to your pleasure. I liked the fact that I was stealing business from strippers.

It turned out also that J. and Celeste had been colluding. I had no idea how they'd got each other's numbers. But they had, and somehow they'd been discussing my career. I didn't mind. Well, not too much. Celeste knew what I did, and I was only slightly wary about the level of detail that she got. But the advantage was that they both knew a lot of people, and so could pass a lot of work my way.

One of my first hen-presents was courtesy of Celeste. A friend of hers, a girl she'd spoken about on a number of occasions but who I'd never met, was getting married. Celeste had drunkenly suggested to her that instead of a piss-up, she should spend her last official night of freedom being professionally pleasured. The girl heard 'pampered', and thought Celeste was sending her to a spa. When Celeste cleared up the misunderstanding and explained about me, the girl, who we can call F., accepted the gift enthusiastically.

Celeste handed over a cheque and the details. Even though she was my friend and my flatmate, she still stuck to protocol, and I was glad. As I've already said, there's a big problem with giving freebies.

The girl lived out of town, in fact in the same village she'd grown up in, with Celeste, somewhere leafy out on the South Downs, and had come up to London to spend the weekend before her wedding. The excuse she'd told her fiancé was that she was having a spa weekend in the city, with some shopping and dining with Celeste and a few buddies thrown in. All that was pretty much true, with the small omission of my services on the Saturday night.

The taxi dropped me on the marble doorstep of a little boutique hotel near the Tate Modern. The glass double doors slid open for me, and I asked the receptionist for the room number of my assignment. She called up to the room and then pointed me to the lift. I clicked across the floor and then went up a couple of floors. The hotel smelt of expensive perfumes and curative oils; I imagined my date spending the day being rubbed, pampered, waxed and massaged, and guessed that all that was missing was some closer attention from me.

I found her room and knocked twice. A husky voice called me in.

I was impressed.

Firstly, the room was spacious and luxuriously furnished. Secondly, on the bed, propped up on her elbows, was Celeste's friend, F. She was shorter than Celeste, a similar age, curvy, with lots of long blonde hair. And she'd dressed for the occasion, better than any normal hen-night outfit: an Agent P. corset, fishnets and crotch-tie knickers. It was an outfit designed for filthy sex. There was also, I noticed, a riding crop on the bedside table.

'Hi. I'm Cesc. Pleased to meet you.'

'I can tell,' she said. She'd noticed that I'd got wood on sight of her.

'So,' I said, hanging my coat behind the door. 'How can I help you?'

'Well,' she replied. 'While I work out what I want you to do, first you can go down on me while I watch porn.'

It was a surprising request, but not one totally out of the blue. A few clients enjoyed porn, and Raven had once played vintage sound recordings of couples fucking during one of our sessions, while she mouthed their old-fashioned cries and moans.

I stripped and worked my way over to F. She was, without doubt, a girl who'd enjoyed too much of a lot of things, including sex, cigarettes and probably money, but she was none the worse for it. With my head between her ankles, I ran my palms up her stockings, and then massaged inside her thighs as I kissed my way up her legs. Greedily, she undid the front of her knickers, and soon the rough elastic of her suspender belt straps was clamped around my ears as I pleasured her pussy with my tongue.

Behind me I heard the sounds of pay-per-view movies: a mix of American and foreign voices in varying states of arousal and sexual excitement. I heard women beg to be fucked in various ways, men praise the sucking skills of their partners and one actress ask in a Texan brogue for 'all your cocks in me, now'. Soon, F. had produced a vibrator, and I was penetrating her with its thick head while I licked away on her aroused clitoris. Meanwhile, the sounds of fucking coming from the television became ever more urgent, as an orgy erupted. I cast a glance over my shoulder as I took a breath, to see a woman on all fours sucking two men while another screwed her from behind, while in a corner another couple looked on, masturbating each other furiously.

F.'s orgasm coincided with the climax on screen. I pushed her further with the vibrator, while quickening the strokes with my tongue, and she began to come with loud gasps and a gush of juices from inside her. I hoped the room was well soundproofed, but soon decided that other guests and staff should expect it. Once she had savoured the last throbs of her climax, she settled back down on the bed and I squatted, admiring her voluptuous form.

With her breath back, she looked at me, and then cast a glance over my shoulder at the pay-per-view behind me.

'I want to do some of that,' she said. I turned and observed an athletic coupling between a muscular stud and a pneumatic blonde. After a few moments, another man joined in, the actress mouthing his penis energetically while bouncing back and forth on the penetration from behind.

'There's only one of me, but we can try,' I said.

I put a condom on and moved her into a position parallel to that of the girl on screen. Then I slid into her, while giving her the vibrator to mouth and taste her own cum. I screwed her with the same, rapid rhythm of the actor, while she, occasionally shooting a look at the screen, sucked off the imaginary third party.

The actress didn't come, and neither did she, but both their cries became more urgent. The image cut, and now the woman was riding her partner, the other man gone. We swiftly switched position, her breasts still held tight in the corset. I noticed two little slits, and freed her hard nipples, sucking them as the man on screen did. Then, from off screen, the other stud appeared, and positioned himself between the couple's legs, behind the girl. He fondled his enormous cock to arousal, tensing his stomach muscles, and with the other hand running juices from her pussy to between the girl's cheeks. Soon, he was entering her as well, her teeth gritted in determination as she received the double penetration. Meanwhile, I moistened the vibrator, and copied the same penetration on F. from behind. She too gritted her teeth, and like the girl on the screen her moans and pleas grew louder. Soon, all of us were coming, F. screaming the same words she heard on screen, while the two men shot their spunk into the actress. My thrusts grew quicker, looking at F., looking at the screen, while my hot juices flowed into her.

As we fell back down onto the bed, the scene on the TV turned into a mass orgy of hot and sweaty sex.

'I don't have any friends with me, I'm afraid,' I said to her.

'Well, we can always play,' she said.

On the screen, a porn star was lying on her back with men screwing her from all angles. Other women were on hand to fluff and suck the guys, while the sexy blonde in the middle groaned and gasped with convincingly feigned pleasure. There was so much action that it was almost impossible to make out how many and who were doing what.

F. turned round onto her back, her head at the end of the bed, leaning over, watching the screen upside down. Her large, round breasts were still considerable, even in that position, her big nipples still poking through the slits of her corset. I found another vibrator and gently placed its three ends in where they were designed to go. The triple stimulation, along with the porn, aroused her immediately. I checked the screen and adopted the pose of one of the men, stationing my legs over her head and deep-throating my cock into her mouth as I lay over her and she watched my balls and the screen, upside down between my legs. The girl on screen was taking multiple penetrations, so I slid the Rabbit in and out while rocking my penis in and out against her tongue. We fucked like that for several minutes, with her watching the porn and taking my dick deep between her lips, while I used the vibrator to pleasure her in multiple ways. Soon she was coming, sucking hard on my penis, her body quivering under me, while my second shot of sperm coursed out of my cock and deep into her throat.

We rested for a while, still watching ever more outrageous films, before a final session from behind, watching another porn movie. I left her, sweaty, exhausted and half dozing, in the early hours of the morning. On the way home, I texted Celeste to thank her for the client, while wondering if there was a way I could get myself included on a wedding list service.

Chapter Thirty-four

As well as wealthy single ladies, frustrated fiancées, and decadent brides-to-be, my Jennies include quite a number of married women. It brings some risks, but in general the women are far too clever and have much too much at stake to risk getting caught. In general, they also have husbands who are away enough to give their wives plenty of time for themselves.

One of my Jennies even introduced me to her husband. She said I was her new hairdresser. My departure had accidentally coincided with his early return from a business trip, and I kept my best, fixed smile without panicking throughout the whole, slightly edgy scene.

Later, she'd told me about the conversation she'd had later with her husband. He said that while he had nothing against homosexuality, he was unhappy about her employing so many gay men, in case it had an effect on their two teenage sons. That she passed on this particular gem as we were deep in the middle of a multi-orgasmic screw made his prejudice and his mistake even more ridiculous and amusing.

I asked her about the marriage thing, about why many apparently happily married women saw fit to employ my services. The Jen in question was a member of Agnes's circle of friends, a forty-something semi-hippy with too much money and time on her hands. Her husband had made a hefty packet in eco-architecture, and appeared to be a charming, handsome and wealthy man. At least in our brief meeting, and what I could gather from the times she mentioned him in passing.

They had three children, and superficially their relationship was about as perfect as a *Guardian*-reading liberal couple's lives can get. Yet underneath her earth-motherly exterior, she spent a lot of time and money on me and on all things sex related. It wasn't quite a double life, rather a part of her life that her husband was looking at but failing to identify, like a colour-blind man looking at a magic-eye picture.

I couldn't manage to understand why he was apparently happy to miss out on the pleasures that his wife had to offer. By her account, they had sex single-figure times a year, certainly no more since they'd had children. It was almost a question of birthdays and Valentines, if she was lucky. It was a miracle, I thought, that the second and third had ever been conceived. But she was a fantastic lover: she could boast some very sexy variants on Pilates moves, was generous when it came to foreplay, seldom declined any suggestion and possessed a remarkable collection of elaborate costumes. Sex with her looked like it was being photographed by Guido Argentini, and was without fail a genuine pleasure. If I'd been looking for an older woman, she would have been a great candidate for the role.

So, I could never quite understand why she was paying for sex. Breaking what is sort of a professional taboo, I even asked her after one particularly elaborate fuck.

'I pay my exercise instructor, I pay my therapist. I pay my cleaner. I'm just being consistent.'

'What about your husband?'

'I don't pay for him. Well, at least not in cash. In fact, if I'm fair, he forks out for rather a lot. Including you, I suppose.'

'No, but I mean, you have kids. He seems like a good

guy. Why don't you just, you know, egg him on a bit?'

'Cesc, are you trying to sack yourself? Don't you enjoy this work?'

'Of course I do. No. I'm just, you know, curious.'

'Christ. Can't you just shut up and fuck?'

'I can, I can,' I said, holding up an apologetic hand. She seemed to relent after a while.

'I'm sorry. Look, my husband is excellent at many things. But sex isn't one of them. He's just never been any good. And I don't want to keep hurting his feelings.'

'What about having affairs?'

'He doesn't. And I've stopped sleeping with his friends. It's too risky. Whereas you, well I can trust you.'

'Because you're paying?'

'Yes. And you have a trustworthy face,' she said, cupping my chin in her hand in a way that was maternal and only slightly disturbing.

I realised that she was right. There is a serious problem out there: a lot of men do not know how to fuck. Not only that, but no one is on hand to teach the very simple things. Like, for instance, the useful fact that in the absence of lubricant, there is a cheap alternative: foreplay. That foreplay, in all its variants, be it massage, games, oral sex, does not need to be seen as some sort of preamble, but as an essential part of the act itself.

And then there's the problem men have with female anatomy. I'll agree that the G-spot can seem like a problem, that after years of scientific research, there's still no conclusive answer that can give men a magic set of coordinates. But I can assure any male reader: the G-spot exists. It has been proven to exist. You can find it. It's just in some cases it's not where you expect it to be. In some cases, the spot that really turns a woman on is

181

nowhere near where you think it should be, or is in the very last place you look. Like in the brain, for example.

If you really can't find it, of course, there's an alternative. It's called the clitoris. But despite the fact that Mother Nature was good enough to put that somewhere it can be seen, it is still too much for many men.

I realised that many of my clients were up against serious cases of male ignorance. A lot of men don't pay attention in biology classes, and then assume that everything is as easy as in Hollywood, where the female orgasm requires nothing but good dentistry and a fast car.

And then there's the problem of selfishness: a lot of men really don't care about women's pleasure, certainly if they've been in a relationship a long time, are too tired to worry about sex or are selfish by nature. That seems to be a lot of men, from what I've been told.

I always think of sex as being like a dinner. You don't rush through your starter and then skip to dessert before your companion has even so much as seen a bread roll. And you don't order four courses if your date isn't eating. You need some self-control, and otherwise, well it's just bad manners.

My feeling is that it's down to a lack of decent education. I was lucky. I had a decent teacher. Agnes's friend reminded me a lot of the woman who taught me an awful lot of what I know.

Chapter Thirty-five

As I said, Agnes's friend reminded me an awful lot of a woman who was very important to me, and I became very fond of her.

She reminds me a lot of an older woman I once knew.

I should just come out and say it. I was taught to fuck by an older woman, a friend of the family, when I was a teenager. Isn't that the best way?

I've thought for a while that it would be a service to humanity, to men and women alike, if these generous and pleasantly perverse women should be hired and sent into colleges or universities as a service to all. There could be a course on it, a sub section of biology, safe sex, sex education or whatever it's called. What women want, or something like that.

I can't remember whether it was a friend of my mother, or the mother of a friend, who took it on herself to teach me about sex. I was at boarding school, my parents away because of one or another of my father's jobs. Boarders had the option to stay at school over the weekend, or, if they could get a note, they could stay at a friend's house. I'd probably just turned eighteen, perhaps, and it was probably the year before I did my A-levels.

It must, I think, have been my friend's mother. We'd been pals for a few years, sharing tastes in music and playing sport together. He was the clever one; I was the sporty one. He helped with my schoolwork; I got his back when we played rugby and football. We'd both had a couple of girlfriends by then, although nothing too serious.

I remember my dad telling me once that his own father had taken him to a brothel when he was about fourteen, but he never did the same for me. I lost my virginity with a girl a couple of years older than me when I was about sixteen. I'm guessing, now, that she must have been a sixth-former from a nearby school, or perhaps it was at one of the awful formal balls we were obliged to attend. The precise details are lost in the haze of hormones and illicit drink. But I was, like almost all teenage boys, inexperienced and fairly incompetent.

My friend's father was away a lot, but his mother was home, unlike my parents who were always travelling around together. So I used to stay round at my mate's family home, a big converted farmhouse in a village near the school. I think in part I was only invited round as a decoy for my friend's own excursions with a girl he knew from the girls' school in town. When asked what he was doing, my friend could say he was going into town to get something for me, or we were going record shopping together. I was happy to play decoy for him, while he snuck off to see his girl, who had fairly liberal parents and didn't mind him spending time in her room.

Now, when I said 'older woman', these things are relative. My friend's mother was quite a lot younger than her husband, and I'm guessing now that she can't have been forty, and may even have been younger. I'm not sure whether she was a second wife, because my friend has a much older sister who lived in London and was seldom around. Whatever the details, there was something like a shadow in the house, and my friend's mother was struggling to escape from under it.

I got the strong impression that she'd married for money and been rather disappointed when that was what she got. She told me very little about herself – she'd worked in the office of her husband; she liked to travel. I had a suspicion she might have been an airhostess once. She was always well dressed, fully made-up and neatly elegant, even first thing in the morning over breakfast. It was a lot of effort to make for a husband who ignored you.

She was, I discovered, also very bored and was looking for someone to play with.

I can't remember precisely who initiated things between us. It was probably her. At school, I'd seen her picking up my friend before I'd met her, and joked with pals about her attractiveness, particularly the slender legs she'd revealed to us all as she stepped out of a little Merc.

Later, at my friend's house, I'd notice her asking me lots of questions over breakfast, about my studies, and what I wanted to do when I was older. I told her I wanted to act, and she told me about her modelling career, which had been brief but successful, although she was, she mentioned a few times, too short to do catwalk. I still see her picture now, in department store promotions and better-quality catalogues.

She didn't seem to mind when her son disappeared out on one invented errand or another, and seemed quite happy sitting watching videos or TV with me. I noticed on later visits that there were awkward occasions. I went upstairs once, and saw her in her underwear through a crack in the bedroom door. I was almost sure she was looking at me, delaying as she pulled up a stocking. Another time, I walked into the unlocked bathroom to see her wearing only a towel. Jokingly, she went as if to flash me. I spun round, embarrassed, and probably blushed to my roots.

Over a few weeks, with me visiting most weekends, I

realised that not only did I have an irreconcilable crush on her but also that she flirted with me a lot. I have no idea whether her son realised or not, but it didn't seem to upset him. He came home once and found us close together on the sofa – I'd sat down first, his mother had joined me. He left us to it, wandering upstairs to talk to another friend on the phone.

It wasn't long, though, before I realised that at least some of my feelings were being reciprocated.

Chapter Thirty-six

It was the last weekend before one holiday or another, and my friend was out, allegedly searching for a spare part for a bike so that we could go for a long ride together on the Sunday – I was training for the annual school race – but really to meet his girlfriend.

I was watching films on TV, while my friend's mother idly flicked through a magazine. I'm not sure whether we were watching satellite, or pay-per-view, but for some reason, there was a sex scene. I was mildly embarrassed and thought about turning over, but I noticed that she looked up and then at me.

'Have you ever been with a girl, Cesc?' she asked.

I was stunned by the question, and thought about lying.

'Erm, yes,' I said. 'Once or twice.'

She gave me a sweet, slightly condescending smile.

'How was it?'

'How do you mean?' I said, gulping with nerves.

'Well, was it like on the movies?' she asked.

I looked up, my cheeks cherry red, and saw an actress coming spectacularly under the thrusting buttocks of one actor or another.

'Not quite like that, I'll admit,' I said, with a nervous laugh.

'Would you like to learn?' she asked.

For a second, I panicked. My head was the temperature of a kettle. My balls had shrivelled. My heart was beating out of my chest.

It was, with hindsight, probably the most important decision of my life.

'With you?' I asked.

'Of course with me.'

'Won't your husband mind?' I asked.

'Not if we don't tell him,' she said.

I nodded. She held out a hand, and led me upstairs to the best classroom of my life.

The first thing she taught me was to appreciate your partner's body. I don't think we even had sex that first time, up in the vast master bedroom she and her husband so seldom shared. We stripped together, very slowly, and she took time to make me get to know her body, her feet, her hands, even her ears, while she did the same to me.

Then we spent a lot of time in our underwear – she was always perfectly done up, and looking back I wonder now whether she might even have done some work as a pro on the side. She kissed me, whispering to me a lot, asking me what felt nice and also telling me what she wanted me to do.

Finally, after what seemed like an age, in which my cock had been straining against my underwear and I'd been nervously trying to stop myself coming prematurely, she stripped, away from me at the end of the bed, and showed me how she liked to pleasure herself. She showed me how she'd tease her nipples, and then she lay face down, massaging the small of her back and her buttocks. And then, best of all, she sat, ankles crossed, facing me, naked, and showed me how she made herself come. I watched her strokes, watched her rub the other hand against her breasts and flat belly, while her head tipped back and she moaned my name in pleasure. She climaxed with quick strokes of her clit, accompanied by deep thrusts with the fingers of the other hand, bouncing up and down and moaning to me in breathy gasps.

Once she'd finished, she looked at me through half-closed eyes, a bead of sweat on her forehead.

'Now show me what you do,' she said.

I realised that it would take no more than a few tugs on my cock to have me coming all over her exquisite sheets, and that might not make a good impression. I tensed all my muscles and put my hand to my erection.

'Stop,' she said, coming closer. My penis was quivering with excitement, and as much as I wanted her near me, I also needed a cold shower and a sit-down in a quiet room.

'Close your eyes,' she said.

I did as she asked.

Soon, she was sitting behind me. I could feel her erect nipples against my back, and her slim hands on my chest and then on my stomach. She wrapped her legs around me and then ran both hands to my groin. She circled around the base of my shaft, gently massaging my balls, and then finally running a hand along the length of my cock, while she cupped my balls with the other. A shot of liquid metal ran through my groin and thighs, and I leant back, gasping with pleasure.

'Just relax,' she said, developing a slow, gentle rhythm. 'I don't want you to come, OK.'

I nodded, wincing with effort, but she was a master technician. Each time she sensed my excitement rising, she stopped and gave a tweak on my balls. She kept this up for what seemed like for ever, each time the pain and joy of the expected climax rising to levels I'd not imagined possible.

And then she stopped.

'I'm going to teach you something about etiquette,' she said. 'Keep your eyes closed.'

I felt her skin leave mine, and then sensed her in front

189

of me.

'The rudest thing you can do is come when it's not welcome. I only want you to come when I say so.'

My eyes tightly closed, I sat waiting for her next move. Suddenly, I felt a delicious spike of pleasure: she was running her tongue against the head of my penis. I arched my back and felt the rush of orgasm, but tensed and held it in. The feel of her tongue was gone.

'Good,' she said. 'Keep that up, and we'll have a great time.'

She used her mouth much as she'd used her hand, bathing me in the most delightful of pleasure, and then stopping me as the sensation became too much for me. She sucked in deep, slow movements, drawing me deep into her mouth and savouring the throb of my penis. And then, with a move and a tweak, she was off me.

'Now,' she said, 'your final lesson for today. And then, if you're lucky, I'll let you come. Open your eyes.'

I opened them. She was lying back in front of me. Her legs were spread, revealing her neat little triangle of hair, while she idly played with her sex.

'I'm going to teach you how to pleasure a woman, if that's OK.'

I nodded, desperately hoping she'd let me come in her mouth. She guided me towards her, instructing me on where to put my tongue, what speed and pressure to use and when to penetrate her. Soon I'd got the hang of it and was enjoying the bittersweet taste of her juices. She came quickly, clearly aroused by the set-up and her earlier orgasm. I lapped enthusiastically at her, and felt a tweak on my hair.

'Don't get carried away,' she said, between gasps. 'No one likes being licked out by a spaniel.'

I concentrated on my tongue work and probed her

clitoris. Soon her climax was well under way, and she bucked under my attentions.

'That's it, yes. Just there,' she shouted at me. As her legs kicked about around me and she pushed me hard in towards her pussy, I continued stroking and licking her. The instructions were over, and she was instead noisily enjoying her orgasm.

Once she'd finished, I sat back, admiring her beautiful naked body and examining my erection. I hadn't come, despite how turned on her orgasm had made me.

'What now?' I asked.

'Well,' she said, lazily propping herself up on an elbow. 'Since you've been a good boy …'

She gently took my penis and guided it towards her mouth. 'You can come now, if you want,' she said, touching her tongue to my tip and then covering it with her lips.

I lasted about three of four strokes before ejaculating in a pulsating stream, my body shaking with pleasure and relief. As I came, she looked me in the eye and almost seemed to smile, keeping my cock deep in her mouth and swallowing every last drop.

She was, I discovered, a woman who was both extremely generous, and completely selfish, and it was a delicious combination.

Chapter Thirty-seven

We saw each other in much the same way for several weeks. In fact, the very next day, once her son, my friend, had gone out with one excuse or another, she suggested we go upstairs where she could show me some old photos from her modelling days. I didn't realise at first that it was just pretence, and she did indeed show me some photos: an album full of lingerie shots taken when she was in her twenties. There was something slightly clumsy about how she looked, and I told her I thought she was sexier now.

She smiled and closed the album.

'You're learning fast. Come on, let's teach you some new tricks.'

That day, she taught me how to fuck.

I'll elaborate.

Again, she stripped, this time keeping her distance from me. And then, gorgeously naked, she disappeared.

'I'm going for a shower. I'll be back. I expect you naked and hard when I'm finished.'

I hurriedly tore off my clothes and threw them towards the door; my cock was already stiff. I stood waiting, and then sat, and then lay, idly playing with myself. I could hear the sound of the shower and I listened for her. After a few moments, I realised that I could hear her, and that low gasps and moans were coming from the en suite.

I stood and walked over. The door was half open, and I could hear the sounds of her coming. I pushed the door slightly, and looked in: in the cubicle, she was standing, legs slightly bowed, masturbating with one hand while pleasuring herself with the hard stream of the shower head, which she held in the other.

She saw me watching her, and continued, looking at me all the time.

'Get back,' she mouthed, in between her moans.

Desperate to join her, but eager to please, I stood a moment before I realised the importance of paying attention to her instructions. Soon, she was with me, drying herself off with a thick dressing gown.

'It's all about patience, you see, Cesc,' she said, stretching out her arms and allowing the gown to drop to the floor. Naked, she was beautiful, firm and slender, her nipples still hard from the shower session. She gave me a twirl and I admired the curve of her buttocks and the little gap at the top of her thighs. 'Where the light of heaven shines in,' she once told me.

'It's all about patience,' she said again. She reached into a bedside cabinet, and produced a condom. 'And being sensible,' she added.

We knelt in front of each other, naked, her hair still wet, my cock rigid in expectation, and, not taking her eyes from mine, she unwrapped the condom and slipped it down me.

'We'll try a few basic positions today. You're not to come until I say so, OK?'

I felt months of tension piling up at the base of my cock as she lay back to welcome me inside her.

'If you feel yourself having trouble, push your tongue to the roof of your mouth and close your eyes,' she said. 'I have a book that will explain why it works, you can have a read if you like.'

Her interruption got me back on track, and I took her advice. She guided me towards her and held me back from full penetration.

'Slowly,' she whispered. 'You're an actor. You know how important a good entrance is.'

I slid into her as slowly as possible, leaning my head back and savouring the pleasure. She ran her hands over my chest and then drew me down to kiss her, our bodies wrapping each other up while I felt her squeeze the muscles of her pussy around me. I was deep inside her, moving only slightly, as she guided me to rub against her while probing her deep inside. It didn't take long for her to begin gripping more tightly, rubbing against me in quick, feathery strokes.

'Don't come,' she whispered breathily in my ear, as she did just that, jolting her head back and hooking her legs around me. As she came, I felt her losing control for the first time, calling out my name and saying, 'Oh fuck, yes.' I sped up my strokes, but the tight grip of her legs around me kept a break on as she savoured the flow of her climax. I tensed every muscle to avoid coming, and soon she had relaxed beneath me.

'We'll do some basic, popular positions today, OK?'

She wriggled out from under me and flipped over onto all fours. There, she instructed me in a series of variants of sex from behind, explaining to me how to judge speed and penetration, the angle of the stroke and when to help her out by playing with her clit. The result was the same as before, and soon she was coming noisily as I pounded methodically from behind her, steeling myself against the onrush of my own orgasm. By the end, her arms had given up and she was flat against the surface of the bed. Once the throes of her orgasm had died down, I lay on top of her, still inside her, my head in her shoulder blades, hearing her heartbeat slow down.

'You can come now,' she said, after a while. I was half hoping for another one of her beautiful blow jobs, but instead she wriggled out from under me and pushed me back into a squatting position. She stood over me, crotch at eye level, and pressed my head towards her. I obediently stuck out my tongue, ignoring the taste of rubbery fruits from the condom. She flicked herself against my tongue, standing legs firm over me, grasping my hair and directing the speed. At the height of her excitement, she pulled away and sexily dropped down into my lap. With a twist, I was inside her, and she leant back and rocked herself to an orgasm. I could feel the pulsation of her climax inside her tight little pussy, and despite my best efforts could no longer control myself. As she rocked hard in my lap, I leant back and felt the intense pain and sudden, glorious release of a climax deep inside her.

That was the second lesson of many.

Chapter Thirty-eight

We continued like that for quite some time. The pattern was almost always the same. I stayed round, allegedly to see my friend. Her son, my friend, would make half-baked excuses to pop out, and then go off to see his young lady. Looking back, I wonder whether he simply thought I was happy at home, reading or watching TV. If he knew what I was up to with his mother, he never let on. I think he was very naive.

Meanwhile, his sexy young mother taught me about sex. She taught me about condoms, about positions, about different types of orgasm and about what you could call the etiquette of sex. She taught me some massage techniques she'd learnt, and even lent me books on sex that she kept in a semi-hidden drawer of the bed, along with a set of handcuffs and a couple of vibrators, which she also taught me how to use.

We didn't just have formal lessons in her bedroom. On a few occasions I surprised her in the kitchen and we ended up making extra-curricular love on the table. Once, she even snuck into my bedroom in the middle of what must have been a particularly lonely night, and sucked me off while I slept. I awoke, half coming, before she climbed on top of me to finish the job.

She taught me a lot of things, mostly out of her own selfish love of pleasure, but also, I think, out of a kind of directionless generosity. Over the years I've asked myself about her a lot. I wondered whether she had slept with other lads from the school, or whether the apparent falling out with my friend's sister might have had something to do with an earlier misdemeanour. But there were no rumours, and no one else seemed to stay round as much as I did. I heard a few years later, on the grapevine, that she and the husband had divorced. He'd been having an affair, and so got taken to the cleaners. I rather lost touch with my friend, and even though I saw his name mentioned in an evening newspaper, attending some charity bash or another, I never thought to call him up. It wasn't really him I wanted to speak to. No, I hoped that maybe I could pick up where I'd left off with his mother, my first proper lover, and my best teacher.

I still remember our final lesson.

She had made me massage her and go down on her until she was almost coming. By then I'd come to love the taste of her pussy, and even to be able to detect different stages of her pleasure. But this time she'd cut me off, and, then, to my surprise, she'd had me kiss and lick around her buttocks, before she taught me some new tricks altogether, before making me return to her clit and lips for a final surge.

After she'd come, I sat back and looked at her. She had a wicked, catlike look in her sleepy eyes. With one hand she was vaguely stroking my erection.

'There are some things,' she said, slowly and luxuriously, 'that you either don't ask for, or you only ask if you know the answer is yes.'

I looked at her, questioningly, admiring her naked body, as she lay across the bed, lighting up a cigarette with the other hand and then smoking into an ashtray on the floor. I was lazily stroking her peachy smooth flanks and hips. My fingers strayed to the cleft between her buttocks.

'Like what?'

'Like whether you can put it there, for example,' she said, raising her eyebrows at me over her shoulder.

'Can I?' I chanced.

'What do you think?'

'Well I've asked, haven't I?'

'A quick learner,' she said, as I slowly slid towards her and to the final pleasure we shared.

That was our last session together. I got a message at school almost completely by surprise that my father had moved appointments, and the new position was attached to a different school. I packed up and changed schools over the holidays.

I didn't see her after that, and in fact I didn't even get a chance to say goodbye to her. It wasn't like I could say to her son, my friend, 'Oh by the way, do you mind telling your mum I won't be able to screw her this weekend 'cos I'm going to another school. And does she have any tips about how to do good threesomes, 'cos we haven't got to that bit yet?' Sometimes I think I look for her in every woman I meet, and other times I realise just how much from her I learnt for this job. Pro or not, she was a consummate professional.

Chapter Thirty-nine

I'll have to apologise for getting distracted again.

But I guess it's important that you know a bit about how I learnt what I needed to know for this job. I'm not saying that my pal's mother taught me everything that I know, but she gave me a good start, and I'm pretty much eternally grateful to her. If I ever saw her again, I know just how I'd thank her.

So I suppose you could say it was three women who got me into this – her, J. and Celeste. Celeste, really, just helps things keep rolling on, coming up with new ideas and finding an occasional client here and there.

I'm glad of the female help, because it's not always a straightforward job, particularly given how crowded the market can be. One evening I was out with Celeste, down in Soho, having a quiet glass of wine on one of my days off. But even as we were chatting about work, with Celeste explaining a fairly elaborate plan she was trying to foist on me for charging corporate rates, I noticed a sexy girl behind her giving me the eye. She was younger than me, small, with a kind of up-market rock chick look. I blame Kate Moss: short kilt, heavy boots, strappy top and harsh haircut and dark dye job. But she had full lips and breasts that were big for her frame: in short, she was built well for a good screw.

After I'd dismissed Celeste's idea and tried to persuade her that only so much interest in my profession was really healthy, she left me, allegedly in search of cigarettes. I caught the little rock chick winking at me, so went over. She was with a girlfriend who was talking on a mobile about some gig or another, paying no attention to our little exchange.

'I noticed you looking at me. Do you want something?' she said.

'Yes,' I said. 'If you do, that is,' I added. It must have been the hot, muggy evening, I thought, making everyone saucy. She raised her eyebrows, gave a wink to her friend and followed me.

Soon we were at the end of an alley, hidden by some bins. Not glamorous, I thought, but just about right for a quick, dirty shag. We kissed, angrily and clumsily, and I slid my hands under her little skirt.

'Naughty,' I said to her. 'No knickers.'

'Easier that way,' she said, her accent half fake cockney, half home-counties public school.

I played with her pussy while she handled my crotch, and soon she had unzipped my fly and was heading down to her knees.

'How much?' she said.

I was shocked.

'You can have this one for free,' I said, leaning back and getting ready to enjoy. But she stopped.

'No. I mean, how much is this worth to you,' she said, one hand on my erect dick, the other on my thigh.

'I'm sorry. I'm not quite sure I follow you,' I said.

'A nosh,' she said. 'It costs.'

'Right, I see. Yes, it costs. It costs *you*. I'm a professional, you know. I should bill you just for holding it. I don't do test drives.'

She stood up and took her hands away from me.

'You're a professional?'

'Yes. And there should be some solidarity between workers, don't you think?'

She shook her head. 'I'm sorry. I've got completely the wrong end of the stick.'

'You're right there,' I said, looking down at my unsatisfied erection.

She walked away down the alley, shaking her head and adjusting her clothes.

'Hey,' I said, 'you're not going to finish what you started?' I thought it was a funny line, but the only response was a raised finger over a shoulder.

Once I'd tucked myself away and done myself up, I sidled back out. The rock chick and her pal had gone, and Celeste was back at the table, smoking urgently.

'That's weird. Where have you been?' she asked.

'Gents,' I said.

'Up an alley?' she asked.

I shrugged.

'Look,' she said, 'I've just had a weird text.' She showed me the message. It was weird.

'Tell your pimp you work for us,' it said.

'That is weird,' I said. 'I didn't know you had a pimp.'

'I'm not a fucking prostitute, Cesc,' she said.

'No. In that case it's even weirder.'

It was, it turned out, also Celeste who got me into the most trouble I've been in since I started this job.

Celeste had got me what on the face of it was a particularly delicious assignment with a young model friend of hers. They'd met while Celeste was helping out (I guess that probably means standing around) on a shoot on the South Bank. Somehow at some stage, she'd told her friend about me and set up the deal.

In fact, it was one of those jobs that sound a lot better than they really are: paid sex with a catwalk model sounds fantastic, but she was probably my most difficult client. She was a posh girl in her early twenties who'd made a fortune by winning a TV modelling competition and successfully fronting a series of high-profile underwear and perfume campaigns. But she was also terribly bored, too skinny, sexually frustrated and quite possibly had a drug problem, all of which made her demanding, unpredictable and not especially gifted in bed.

I tried my best with her, but I suppose that mostly she was paying me for discretion. I wasn't even convinced that she enjoyed sex. Once she'd come, she had little or no interest in anything else. I don't have to come with a client, but only the most selfish of Jens actively avoid it. Even when subject to my best attentions she'd become distracted, and once even wandered off to make a phone call halfway through an orgasm. Hers, I hasten to add.

The rest of this story comes with an admission. Remember how I said that I don't go with other men? Well it's not totally true. After about three or four sessions with this particular Jenny – let's call her Niamh – I tried to find out what it was she'd really like.

She thought for a moment, puffing on one of the slim, all-white cigarettes she smoked.

'I'd like to be spit-roasted,' she said.

I closed my eyes for a moment, trying to avoid laughing at her use of the term.

'A threesome?'

'Yeah. My boyfriend said he wanted to do it.'

'But what would you like?'

She shrugged.

'I'd like to have a go.'

So, just so you're not too shocked, my confession is that I have been involved in threesomes involving other men. But I always try to avoid getting too close, as short circuits are risky, you know. You've seen *Ghostbusters*, right?

Anyway, that same session she texted her supposed boyfriend. It turned out that he wasn't in fact the man her publicist had her seen with at launches and premieres, but an old boyfriend from the wrong side of town back home, a tough local lad going nowhere fast, who she still saw on the sly. It was, in a way, quite touching. I couldn't quite work out where I fitted into her complicated sex life.

Sometime between the set-up and the date, I got a strange message – a blank envelope posted through the letterbox, without an address or a name. I opened it, and scrawled on the paper was a simple message.

'Your bitches work for us.'

I showed Celeste. She agreed that it was even weirder than her text, but also that it was pretty frightening. I said it was a bit rude to talk about her like that. She gave me a dirty look. Eventually, I decided to ignore it as the work of a freak, and to keep my head down and concentrate on my work.

Chapter Forty

After the two strange messages, I noticed a few other strange things that week: a big black BMW I'd never seen before parked on the street below the flat, whose driver never seemed to go anywhere. Also, I kept bumping into a big guy with a shaven head, in dark glasses and a suit, in several places around town. But there were no more messages, and I wondered whether it was a case of mistaken identity.

I saw Niamh for our special session. We met in a small but extremely plush hotel in Chelsea, up a side street and hidden behind darkened reception doors. I asked for her at reception – she had the penthouse suite under an assumed name, which Celeste had passed on earlier. Niamh was between assignments, and judging by the state of the once beautiful living room of the suite that she and her secret boyfriend seemed to have set about trashing, she had decided to spend her time off boozing, eating junk food and possibly breaking quite a few laws relating to controlled substances. But she was more pleased to see me than usual, and with a silk sheet knotted around her like a post-modern toga, with barely out-of-bed hair and smoky eye make-up, she was sexier than I'd expected.

'My boyfriend's here. Do you want to meet him? Chad, do you want to meet Franco, he's a friend of Cellie.'

I couldn't quite work out why she got everyone's names wrong, but from the bedroom Chad emerged on cue. He was a pale-skinned, shaven-headed gym junkie in sweat pants and vest who looked like he spent all day shifting tyres and heavy car parts, but he was also strangely pleased to see me, dishing out a big high five and a series of elaborate handshakes.

'Fran man, you ready to do this?'

I nodded. 'It's what I do.'

Chad gave a raucous laugh and even Niamh giggled to herself – she seldom laughed.

'Come on then, let's do it,' said Chad, enthusiastically.

As we headed through the white double doors into the wide bedroom, Niamh held both our hands. Before we'd reached the bed, she was pushing off Chad's vest while I removed her sheet-toga and began to massage her little breasts. We positioned ourselves on the bed, Niamh in the middle, facing Chad, with me behind her. I threw off my T-shirt and pressed against her, reaching round to play with her while she began to go down on Chad. I pushed her hips up so that I could lick her from behind, trying to ignore the thumbs-up gesture and broad grin that Chad periodically cast in my direction.

She was perfectly waxed – I'm guessing a condition of the profession – and licking her was a pleasure. She made very little sound, only the occasional whimper and wincing noise to let me know she was enjoying herself. As I pleasured her, I hitched off my trousers and shorts and found a condom, ready for the main event.

I noticed in front that Chad was going for it. He had Niamh's hair firmly grasped in his hands and was thrusting into her mouth, while she was reaching under him to play with his balls. Then her hand slipped back and she began to finger her clit as I licked her from behind.

With her pussy now dripping and Chad leaning back, eyes closed, struggling to contain himself, I decided that it was time. I slipped on the condom and used two fingers to guide myself in her. She gasped and, I think, may have bit Chad's dick as I penetrated her. He looked up and gave me another grin, while I held Niamh's slim hips and worked her from behind. The orgasm she'd begun on my tongue didn't take long to happen, and the sight of me screwing his girlfriend and the sound and sensation of her orgasm seemed to inspire Chad. Soon both of them were coming, Chad shooting into her mouth, while she let out muffled moans and called out my name.

Chad fell back on the bed while I carried on working away at Niamh from behind. With her hands free, she planted her arms, allowing me to tease her nipples and clitoris from behind, soon bringing her to a second orgasm. By now she seemed to have forgotten about her boyfriend, and was looking at me strangely over her shoulder.

'Tell me what you want,' I said.

'Let's swap round,' she said. I pulled out and she rolled over and round. She gripped my penis and mouthed it fully, seemingly enjoying the taste of her own juices on the rubber. I looked at Chad, giving him a thumbs-up, just as he'd given me. He gave me a rather forced smile, and with some effort, fluffed himself up to a second erection and shoe-horned himself into Niamh from behind.

'I can see that's why you're the professional, man,' he said. Niamh gave a sort of muffled laugh that vibrated pleasurably down my shaft. Chad was clearly not being paid for his services, and pounded away mechanically at her from behind, knocking her head against my stomach a few times, before coming, tensing his muscles and staring at her arse in concentration. I held off, even as her sucking grew more intense. Once he'd finished, Niamh moved back.

'Go on, you can come now,' she said.

'Hey Chad,' I said to my fallen comrade. 'I think you owe her one.' He sat up and nodded enthusiastically. Soon, he was working his fingers over her shaven pussy, pleasuring her clit and lips, and fingering her where he'd just come. As she became more aroused, I reached down and pulled on her pointy nipples, and with the peak of her third orgasm I relaxed and let her sucking bring me to climax, holding her firmly by the scruff of the neck as I ejaculated into the condom deep in her mouth.

The three of us fell back on the bed. Chad started clapping. Niamh reached around on the floor for some cigarettes.

'Smoke?' she said.

'Good work, man, good work,' said Chad, taking a smoke from his girlfriend. Of the three of us, he seemed most pleased with the scenario. It was clearly his idea – Niamh had gone along with it, and seemed to have taken pleasure from it, but I realised that she was a malleable girl, and finding out what she really wanted would have been a long and difficult project, possibly even beyond me.

I took my money and left them – Niamh was phoning someone to organise a delivery of something that might have been pizza, or something else altogether. As I walked out of the hotel, giving a thumbs-up to the porter, while wondering whether I wanted to make Niamh a pet project, I noticed that both the black BMW and the big man in the sit were outside.

I stopped, within eyeshot of the hotel, and called Celeste.

'Celeste, are you alright?' I asked.

She sounded like I'd interrupted her at a bad moment.

'Yes. Why? What do you want?'

'Nothing strange going on that I should know about?'

'No. Look, can you call later?'

I hung up and surveyed the scene. It was definitely the same car, and it was definitely the same thug. Luckily, a taxi passed almost immediately, and I hailed it and ducked inside. I had the driver take me on a long route, passing by a friend's house and even stopping for a few minutes outside Archie's flat by the Heath. Although the BMW followed at first, at some stage it must have dropped off, or got lost, and so by the time I got home I had lost my tail.

Chapter Forty-one

Back at the flat, Celeste was hiding away in her bedroom. I checked a few texts, updated a few things on my website and sorted out the details of a couple of assignments. My efforts with Niamh and Chad, the most demanding secret celebrity couple in Christendom, had worn me out, and once I'd showered I found myself dozing in front of a wildlife documentary. The life of a call boy is not all rock 'n' roll and non-stop parties, let me add.

As I dozed, I found myself drifting off into a weird semi-daydream about Niamh and her life, something like the orgy scene in *Eyes Wide Shut*. The switch was that it involved people with familiar faces, including the big thug in the suit and a couple of Celeste's boyfriends. It was a strange image: a vast dark gothic hall, halfway between a Cathedral and the stateroom of a royal palace, and I was standing there, naked, in a wide arc of other men, about twenty in total. Some of us, myself included, had on Venetian carnival masks. In front of us, a few women were lined up: Celeste, Niamh, J., a couple of other clients. There were other women too, wearing masks. All of them had long satin robes in a deep shade of purple.

It worked like this: we stood still, facing each other, and in turn, on cue from an invisible voice, the women would each pick one, or two, or even three of us. The powerful female voice from somewhere off stage then instructed the men to make themselves erect. They did, and then the men were either led away or rejected. I was chosen, weirdly, by Celeste, along with an older guy I've never met before. She simply pointed at him, and then at me.

On instruction from the invisible voice, and with a few strokes of the hand, my cock stood to attention. I was led away by a tall, slim woman, masked and robed like the others. From her body shape, I thought she might be Niamh, but I couldn't be sure: she had long, slim legs, her robe clung to her pert buttocks and her shoulder blades were almost showing through her robe. She took me out of the hall and up a wood-panelled, carpeted stairway, leading to a long corridor of rooms over the main hall. As she walked up the stairs, I admired her ankles and wondered what pleasures awaited.

She showed me a door, opened it, and I passed through into a side room, the other man following me in. Celeste was waiting for us. She slipped off the robe and I saw her naked apart from the tiniest of black G-strings. We've been on beach holidays together, and I've seen her pretty much naked on a few occasions, but in the dream the sight of her slim figure so barely covered turned me on even more. Alongside me, the older man, wearing a black and white harlequin mask, was playing with himself as Celeste reclined on a velvet coach.

Celeste gestured to him, a 'come hither' signal, and he walked over to her. I couldn't see the mask I had on, only the round eyeholes through which I was staring. Celeste leant forward and began to suck the man's dick. I could only see his buttocks, pumping away, with her small hands reaching round to grip them, her mass of hair visible the other side of him.

After a while, the man turned round and gestured with his head for me to join them. I was uneasy about a threesome involving my flatmate, but given the circumstances, didn't quite feel able to resist. As I approached, I could see through the glass arches into other rooms, and over the reclining Celeste down into the hall. Alongside us, groups of people were fucking frantically: an energetic threesome to my right, and next door, two couples were both screwing while watching the other two screw. Down below, in the hall, a mass orgy had broken out: there were couples and threes and moresomes rutting on sofas and on the thick carpet; in every case, the women were outnumbered by men.

The sight aroused me even more, and I stepped forward, hoping Celeste would take me in her mouth with the other man. But as I leant in, I felt a sudden blow to the side of my head.

It was Celeste. Not the Celeste of the dream, but the real-life Celeste, who had hit me round the head with a pillow.

'You randy bastard. You're insatiable.'

'What?' I said, shocked and disorientated by being suddenly awoken. Celeste was perched over me, feet on the sofa, almost the exact reverse of the position she'd adopted with me and the other man in the dream.

'You've just been on a date, and you're having a dirty dream on my sofa.'

I checked my position: I was leaning back, erection clearly visible in my trousers, and had been about to thrust in my sleep. Caught red-handed, or rather, erect-dicked.

'You'll never guess what I was dreaming about,' I said, smiling.

'I don't want to know, you grubby …'

I'd like to say that she was interrupted by a knock at the door, but it would be truer to say that the door collapsed.

We both turned, as a deafening crash invaded the flat. 'What the …?' I began.

In the space where the doorframe had been, I could see the big thug and someone who looked rather a lot like the driver of the BMW. The big man dropped the massive wall-banger he'd used to smash in the door, and pulled out a rubber cosh from inside his suit coat. Celeste screamed and hid behind me.

From outside in the corridor, there came a voice.

'Mr Aleixandre, I presume,' it said. It sounded Eastern European, perhaps Russian.

'Yes. Who the hell are you?'

The third man was smaller than the other two, also smartly dressed, all in black, with his dark hair neatly gelled back. He didn't need to tell me what he did for a living, or, more precisely, what the people who had to work for him did for a living.

Nor did I need him to tell me that I was in big trouble.

Chapter Forty-two

There were a few moments of silence, broken occasionally by the sound of falling carpentry.

I eyed the intruders; Celeste whimpered quietly behind me, and the little pimp gave me a long, satisfied grin.

'Let me guess, Frenchy. Training her up as well?'

'I'm sorry?' I said, after a pause.

'We know what you do, Mr Aleixandre. These poor girls, exploiting them like you do.'

His accent was as thick as borscht, but more difficult to understand was what on earth he was on about. I narrowed my eyes and tried to make sense of what seemed to be a very strange accusation.

'Sorry, Mr, erm, Mr, what is your name?'

'You can call me Wilson.'

'Wilson?' I repeated.

He nodded.

'Sorry, look, I'm not sure what I'm being accused of here.'

'Wilson' turned to his men. On cue, they ran at me, while Celeste ran for her bedroom, slamming, locking and then, by the sounds of things, heavily barricading the door.

Struggling was useless: the big man was a monster, and without needing to use his weapon, he had me in an iron grip in seconds. The other man grabbed my kicking feet and in seconds I was hoisted bodily into the air.

'What the fuck do you want?' I managed to shout.

'Please, my French friend, there's no need for foulness.'

'Look, I'm not fucking French, what's this about?' I said as they carried me to the window.

'Oh shit,' I shouted, as the window was opened. Soon, I had a view of the street: upside down, held by the ankles, suspended over the pavement to the disbelief of passers-by below. I launched into a tirade of swearing and abuse, flailing my arms about in an attempt to strike a blow or catch a grip on anything that wasn't air.

'Please don't struggle, Mr Aleixandre,' said the pimp. 'This is simply a message. From now on, your girls work for us, OK?'

'OK, OK,' I said, still not quite knowing what I was agreeing to. But in a second, I was back inside, dropped on my head and dazed, before the men hurried out through the open door.

'What on earth did he mean,' I asked myself, as the stars began to clear from in front of my eyes, 'my girls?'

After a while, I heard the sounds of hasty deconstruction coming from Cel's room. She emerged, patting her hair and trying to look calm.

'They're gone, right?' she said, breathlessly.

'Yes. You really are a coward.'

'They could have done anything to me.'

I grumbled to myself and struggled to my feet.

'What do you think they wanted? What was he talking about, "your girls"?' I asked her.

'I think I know,' she said. 'He thinks I'm a prostitute. He thinks your clients are prostitutes. And that you're a pimp.'

'What?' I said in disbelief. 'This is all because you look like a posh hooker?'

'Thanks, Cesc. Thanks a lot. I don't, anyway. But some of your girls do.'

I thought for a second. She was right. I'd suspected

214

that J. might have been an ex-pro, and that Raven could very easily carry out the same services she demanded from me on other men for a significant fee. And I didn't want to imagine the sort of things Niamh might do to seal contracts, in her bored and expressionless sort of way.

'This is a problem, isn't it? Do you think that a simple explanation would do?'

Celeste gave me a cold look.

'They'll be back. And you can't give them what they're after.'

'Well obviously. Because they've got the whole thing on arse over head.'

I looked around the room, wondering if there was anything I could use to defend myself in case they called again. I weighed up my chances with a cricket bat against the two thugs.

'How long do you think they've been tailing me for?'

'I saw that car a couple of weeks ago, I suppose,' said Celeste. And then, reluctantly, she looked up and told me.

'They spoke to me first.'

'What?' I said.

'I didn't want to tell you. They'd been following me for a while. First they told me to tell you that I work for them. But I didn't know what they were talking about. So I didn't say anything. They're obviously idiots as well as thugs.' Celeste wiped a tear away from her eye. It had obviously been an emotional few days.

'Shit,' I said. 'This could put me out of business.'

'Cesc, I think business is the least of your worries.'

Luckily, Celeste had insurance, so we had the door fixed that afternoon, as well as calling in a locksmith to fit some heavier bolts and a set of massive bars down both sides of the frame on the flat and the street door. Celeste phoned a couple of friends of hers, and I called a couple of clients, keeping details to the minimum, to make sure no one else had had a similar visit. Fortunately, it seemed the thugs had kept their attentions to a minimum.

Celeste and I talked about the thugs. After much discussion, we concluded that they must be local and perhaps pretty small scale newcomers: Mr So-Called Wilson was menacing me, who he thought was a small-time pimp, and he only had a standing crew of three. But even if they were small-time, they were a lot bigger-time than me. Cricket bat or no cricket bat, I needed help.

Chapter Forty-three

I tried to carry on as normal that week, while thinking through a plan.

It was difficult; I cancelled a session with Agnes, claiming a head cold, as I thought that her genteel, arty world really didn't need this sort of interruption. I thought about asking J. for some advice, but decided that she'd be safer not knowing. Or worse, if she knew, she was ballsy enough to try to do something about it, and I didn't need vigilante clients. I saw Raven's friend, Julia, and was particularly savage in carrying out her instructions.

I got a call from Niamh that week, oddly just as I was standing in front of a large picture of her naked body covered only by a perfume bottle on a billboard in Camden. The thugs had stopped following me, presumably because they knew where to come. Her call was to arrange another date.

'Hi, Chesky. Same time, same place,' she said.

'Uh huh, ' I agreed.

'Chad wants, you know, another session, OK?'

We agreed the details of the date: this time, Chad wanted to play voyeur, watching from another room. I was perfectly happy with the arrangement, provided there were no more violent interruptions.

I took a taxi to the hotel – the same one as before, where it seemed that Niamh and her pals had taken up near permanent residence, particularly now that she'd been made the face of a new big-money perfume launch.

The porter and the receptionist gave me a polite nod and I went up without prompting. The suite, I noticed, had benefited from a clean-up, as if Niamh was expecting guests. Which, in a way, she was. The pizza boxes and vodka bottles had been tidied away. She greeted me at the door, even planting a peck on my cheek. She was in her underwear, sexy stuff, clearly an outfit to impress: an acid bright bra and thong set with hold-ups and kitten heels. The extra height made her taller than me, and she stood back and spread her arm in a star shape.

'Ta-da!' she announced.

That's the thing with underwear: what's better than being well dressed is being well undressed. The very minimum of clothes can take great amounts of time and money: it's what a garment suggests of the rest of the outfit that has been removed that counts. Niamh had hit the note just about perfect.

I clapped and smiled: it was childish, but at least today she was enthusiastic. I caught a movement out of the corner of my eye and noticed another tall girl, crossing into the bedroom.

'A friend,' mock-whispered Niamh. 'You haven't seen her.'

I nodded, wondering whether she was drunk. Regardless, her outfit turned me on, and it wasn't long before we were through in the bedroom. Chad, I noticed, appeared from another room, and then crossed through into the dressing room, off the bedroom, where he sat, watching us through the half-closed door; the other girl – a more voluptuous, olive-skinned colleague of Niamh's – sat on his knee and stroked his neck and shoulders.

Niamh was at her best: we prodded and tickled each other as she pulled off my shirt and trousers, and then without prompting she pushed me back down and began sucking me, casting an occasional glance towards the dressing room. I noticed that the other girl was performing the same task on Chad, crouched down between his legs, her thong pulled up high, tight in the cleave of her sexy arse.

I spun Niamh round so that her crotch was over my face and slipped aside the expensive silk and lace of her little thong to leave her pussy open for my tongue. I licked and probed while she put a flavoured condom on me and then took my cock deep into her mouth, playing with my balls and tightening the pressure around the base. I closed my eyes and tensed, continuing to pleasure her with my tongue.

In the other room, I heard a groan, and looked to see Chad grimacing as he came into the mouth of the girl at his feet. I winked at him and he struggled a smile in response. After just one and a half sessions, I was beginning to think of him as an old, if slightly annoying, friend.

Once he'd finished his orgasm, and Niamh was getting closer to hers, I pushed her up, rolled out from under her and, to her surprise, yanked down her knickers. From behind her, I put my knees down on them, between her legs, half trapping her, and then with a hand across her back and another between her legs, slid into her quickly and fully. She let out a gasp, and it only took a dozen or so strokes before I could hear the beginning of her orgasm. I looked over at my audience and could see the other girl writhing around in Chad's lap as he stroked her clit and toyed with her breasts. I wondered if I might be able to make all four of us come at once.

Niamh's cries were rising, matched by those of the girl in the other room, when once again I was interrupted by the sound of a crashing door.

'Oh fuck,' I shouted. 'Not again.'

I pulled away from Niamh and rolled off the bed.

'Quick,' I shouted, 'come with me.'

I grabbed her hand as she struggled to pull on her knickers, and we stumbled into the dressing room, half knocking over Chad and his other girl.

'Man, what the fuck is this?' he said, standing up angrily and pulling his baggy jeans and boxers up to cover himself.

'Shit. I'm sorry, look, I'll explain,' I said, covering myself while trying to hold up an appeasing hand. I realised I still had the condom on, and picked it off.

'Che, get that shit away from me man,' said Chad. The girls started to shout too, but both were cut off by the sounds of smashing from the next room.

'I can explain. They think I'm a pimp.'

Niamh and Chad both gave me variants on a bewildered look, mouthing my words back to me.

'I'm not. It's basically a massive fuck-up.'

'Too right,' said Chad.

Niamh looked at the door.

'Maybe if I go and talk to them,' she said.

'No way,' said her friend.

There was a knock on the cupboard.

'Delay them, man,' whispered Chad.

'OK,' I said. 'I'm coming out,' I shouted to the intruders, pulling on a pair of jeans I saw lying in a corner of the room.

I opened the door and poked my head out, expecting to be greeted by a fist or a bullet.

Neither. But the three thugs were there again. And they were looking for me.

220

Chapter Forty-four

I surveyed the scene. This time, it looked like a pickaxe had gone through the door, before smashing a TV and a few bits of furniture. It was now lodged in the escritoire under the window in the living room. I didn't want to imagine the scene downstairs.

'Is there really any need for all this?' I asked the slick-haired man.

'If you continue to defy us, we will do what is necessary to protect our interests. Have the girl come out,' answered Wilson.

I looked behind me. Niamh and her friend were cowering behind the door. I couldn't see Chad. Niamh's friend came out, having found a dressing gown to cover her saucy outfit.

'I'm Valentina. What the fuck do you want?' she said. I winced at her aggression, hoping they wouldn't start taking it out on people.

'Well, Miss Valentina. Your pimp is out of business. You work for us now.'

She gave me a look, her black eyes flashing with rage, and tossed her mane of dark hair.

'I'm not a prostitute. And he's not a pimp. I'm a model.'

'Sure,' he said. Then turning to me he added, 'What are you doing Frenchy, training her too?'

'I'm not French. And she's a client. Seriously, guys, come on. Why don't you fuck off.'

'Oh, I see, of course,' said Wilson. 'Andrei, deal with her.'

The big driver stepped forward, heading for the girl. I

stepped in front of her and held my hands up, fully aware that it might be my last heroic act.

'Look, look, I'm sorry. I didn't mean that. But this is ridiculous. Let me explain.'

The big man paused momentarily, confused it seemed. Wilson didn't answer, and I took advantage of the silence to plead my case.

'You've got this totally wrong. I'm the prostitute, not the girls.'

'You. Prostitute?' asked Wilson, his accent barely intelligible now.

'Yes. I mean, I prefer call boy, it's a much nicer term. But that, in essence, is the deal. All these girls you think are my prostitutes are not. They're my clients. Apart from Celeste, of course. But that's a whole different story.'

Wilson thought for a second, and then the cold smile returned to his face.

'Good. Well I not sexist. In that case, you work for us, you are our bitch.'

'Shit, look, that's ridiculous. I can't work for you,' I pleaded.

'You can die, instead,' said Wilson. 'Or we cut off tool of trade, if you like.'

'No, just, come on, be sensible.' I could see the big man stepping towards me, and thought I caught a flash of metal inside the driver's jacket.

'Now look, that's just not going to work,' I said, realising that I could hear the begging tone in my own voice. 'Oh fuck.'

The big man was upon me in a second, while Valentina began to scream. I saw the knife in the driver's hand, and tried to struggle desperately against the big man's grip. I was trapped. And they were going to cut my cock off.

I felt the sweat on my brow and the beat of my heart as Wilson stood over me.

'So. You decide, Frenchy,' he said, while his driver waved his shiny blade in figure of eights in the air.

'No one would touch me if they knew I was employed by organised crime. That's part of the attraction. I'm independent.'

I couldn't stall them any longer. I prepared to beg. And then I heard the shot.

At first I thought I'd been killed, partly because in the confusion the big man dropped me. The force of the landing winded me, and I may even have passed out for a moment. Around me, I heard the sounds of fighting and swearing. As I struggled to pull myself to my feet, I was knocked back down again. I pulled myself out of the way, to the side of the bed, and tried to work out what was going on.

What was immediately clear was that there were a lot of people in the room, and they were all fighting. Two men were grappling with the big thug in the suit, while another had grabbed the driver and wrestled him to the floor. Across the room, someone had bundled Wilson to the floor, and the pseudonymous pimp was shouting and cursing in a language I don't speak.

It was a brief fight. Chad joined the fray, laying into the big man with punches to the stomach and chest until he was crumpled in a huge heap on the floor. Someone else hit the driver with a chair. Even Valentina joined in, spitting and slapping at the driver as he lay defeated on the floor. Two men dragged Wilson across the floor. One of them handed something to Chad. As soon as I realised what it was, I realised I had to step in.

'No, Chad. Don't. And certainly not here,' I said. He

turned, clicked the knife away and went to his back pocket. 'This instead,' he said, waving a heavy black gun at me.

'No, definitely not that. No one is getting either stabbed or shot here. This is a nice hotel.'

Chad turned to the pimp.

'You're a lucky man. I should kill you, you know. Now if I ever hear of you around, I'm gonna find you and I'm gonna mess you up. And all your boys as well. Now get the fuck out!' he screamed.

The three hoodlums picked themselves up and slunk away. I looked over at Niamh, who was laughing rather nervously, scrabbling around in the mess of the bedroom looking for cigarettes. Meanwhile, I got a chance to examine my rescuers: five or six hefty young men, generally younger than Chad, in similar leisure wear and tattoo combinations.

Niamh explained it all to me once the boys had gone. It turned out that Chad wasn't just a gym body with a menial job. Oh no. The pecs and the tats were part of a whole different set-up, because Chad just so happened to be a very significant player in certain, let's say, markets, and the reason Niamh kept him quiet and chose to date celebrities in public was not that he was a nobody, but rather that he was a very big somebody, just not the right type of somebody.

Meanwhile, such was Chad's particular line of work that he was obliged to travel at all times with some cover on hand, a little gang of paid bodyguards. I'd noticed them outside the hotel, and just assumed they were local hoodlums. Little did I know that they'd save my manhood, and that my chat with the thugs had been the delay that Chad needed to call in the hooded cavalry.

Niamh paid me double for the session, which was

generous. We agreed that we could do with a couple of weeks off. Meanwhile Chad gave me a number, and made it very clear that if I ever had any similar problems, he could get them dealt with. I hoped it was a number I'd never have to call.

Chapter Forty-five

I saw Celeste back at the flat and told her the, well, I suppose you could say good news.

She was almost as traumatised by my experience as I was, and after a brief discussion we agreed that it would be a good idea to get away for a week or so. She had some savings, and a few of my clients were away on holiday, so we decided that we could both afford it.

For once though, my luck really was in. I called V. – you remember, the horsy one with the sex toys business – and told her that I'd have to cancel.

'What a pity. Why?'

'I've had a bit of a sticky spot. I think I need to try to get away for a few days.'

'Really? Well I might just have the perfect solution for you.'

It was, I'll admit, a brilliant idea: she was celebrating a particularly successful year for her company, and had decided to invite a whole bunch of her 'people', as she called them, to her villa in the south of France. There would even be a few members of the, shall we say, more select press, helping to promote her website.

'I'm flattered, but why me?' I asked.

'Well, look, you've tried out pretty much everything I've ever sold. And I think you might have some fun.'

'Can I bring a friend? Celeste, my flatmate?'

'Provided she doesn't cramp your style,' she said.

I looked up at Celeste, who was lying with a wet flannel on her forehead, still, she claimed, recovering.

'No danger of that,' I said.

So, the deal was done. As far as any of the guests

were concerned, I was a sex therapist who'd trained at the University of Barcelona and in the States, specialising in the use of specialist aids in overcoming sexual inhibitions. It was suitably ridiculous, and also meant that Celeste was officially my co-researcher, after she'd refused to travel as my official girlfriend.

The next day, there were e-tickets in my inbox and an address in France. Celeste and I booked a car online, upgrading to something ridiculously overpowered to celebrate our free trip. I kept my head down for a few days, printed out a few maps and other bits of information, including some enticing pictures of V.'s villa, and then that Friday Celeste and I headed to the airport.

We left London and rolled out to Gatwick on the rickety local train, Celeste's bags filling much of our compartment – yes, the train was so old it had compartments – and drawing disapproving stares from our fellow travellers. Celeste had panicked repeatedly about the alleged unpredictability of the weather, and the nature of the trip. Both of us had to look like holidaying professionals, rather than a hired shag and his underemployed best friend. As a result, she seemed to have packed everything she owned.

On arrival, Gatwick looked like a cross between a refugee camp and the platform for the last train out of a disaster zone. Long-haul flights were delayed, and families had set up home on the benches and floors all around us. I've always wondered about that: if you're going on a week's holiday, surely after a day or so you'd just sack the trip off and claim the insurance? But the Brits are stayers, after all.

As we queued to drop our bags, I also noticed that it was clearly the day to start a boozy trip away: around us that morning, gangs of stag and hen dos were boozing freely, in silly hats and matching T-shirts. There were also big family groups, and little children on wheelie shoes threaded their way through the crowd with varying degrees of precision while their parents shouted vainly after them. It was, I felt, a very good day to look foreign and smile.

While airports bring out a whole load of bad memories and childhood bogies, they do have one big plus: I've always loved stewardesses. I travelled a lot as a kid, and as in general I was with my father, who was on diplomatic business, we travelled in style. The higher the class of travel, the sexier the stewardess, and the more devoted her attentions.

Celeste chatted away, complaining about the people, the smell and the noise, while I ignored her, watching the gangs of neatly dressed, well made-up, be-suited girls go past. I found myself drawn to the little Korean hostesses, with their starched neckerchiefs flying out at a comical angle, or the slim, elegant and terribly unfriendly French girls in their rich blue suits.

After security and passport control – where they'd demanded I remove my hat, I'm not sure why – we strolled through to the gate. Celeste left me, to visit duty free, where she bought several gallons of perfume and another pair of Ray-Bans, allegedly as presents, although she couldn't specify quite who they were meant for. Then she disappeared again, looking for somewhere to smoke, while I held the fort and waited for boarding.

As it turned out, my luck was in. With seats filling up around me, one of the French air stewardesses came and sat down almost next but one to me. I was leafing through a newspaper, and as she sat down I smiled. I find it impossible not to smile at cabin crew. She gave me a slightly embarrassed look, as if she was in the wrong place, or didn't quite know where she was going and was afraid to ask.

'I'd ask you what you're doing here,' I said, 'but it's a stupid question. Would you like a bit of the paper?'

She turned to me and gave me a quizzical but not unpleasant look. She was my age, with light brown hair swirled up into her little hat, and her tailored uniform hugged a slender, very French body. I noticed little details: the elegant little pearl earrings, the absence of any rings, the perfect line of her lip-gloss on a full, pouty mouth. I thought of Vanessa Paradis' taller sister, if she has one.

'Where are you travelling?' she asked, in crisp, educated English.

'Avignon. City of Popes,' I said. She smiled again. 'You?'

'I'm going home.'

'Working?'

'No, just travelling back.'

'That's good of them. You must be demob happy.'

She gave me another questioning look. 'I've heard that expression. Where are you from?'

'It's long and complicated, and not very interesting. I'm from London, but I'm also sort of Spanish and sort of Argentinian.'

'Hablas español entonces?' she asked me in Frenchified Spanish. I laughed, and answered, and we chatted fairly pointlessly in Spanish for a while. She laughed about my accent, which she said she'd only heard on tapes in class, and I explained it was just a product of too much travel. With Celeste nowhere to be seen, and a line of red 'Delayed' notices on the board in front of us, I suggested we get a drink, and she gratefully

229

accepted.

It was a strange conversation, but fun. We'd both travelled a lot, and had quite a lot in common. We flitted in between English, Spanish and I tried some of my schoolboy French, which basically amounted to me talking in Spanish with a French accent. After one G&T it made her giggle, after two, she found it hilarious.

We were perched on bar stools at the fairly unpleasant bar in the corner of departures, our legs close together and with frequent brushes of hand and knee. Our flights were still delayed, and I bought some more drinks. While I was at the bar, I noticed a couple of fairly leery drunks paying her predictable attention, and on my return suggested we try somewhere else.

'We can go to my lounge. It looks like we'll be waiting a while,' she said.

We necked the drinks – I was starting to feel at least tipsy, while she gave a little stagger, half joking, as she stepped off her stool – and headed upstairs.

I was expecting the question, and as we passed through the sliding doors of the executive lounge with barely a nod to the receptionist and settled onto a wide leather sofa, it came.

'Cesc, you never told me what you do?' she asked.

'Do you want the story, or the truth?' I said, after a pause.

She smiled. 'Oh both, of course.'

I told her about my assignment and the trip to France, explaining my work as a researcher into sexual therapies. She laughed, with a slightly cynical air, throughout my story.

'That's brilliant,' she said, looking away from me. 'But what's the truth?'

'The truth is I fuck for money.'

Her English momentarily let her down. She looked blankly at me.

'I'm a male prostitute.'

'Are you homosexual?' she asked.

'Not with men. My clients are women.'

Her sculpted eyebrows raised and she sat back next to me.

'Wow. You're a gigolo!'

'I prefer not to use that term.'

'Are you good?' she asked.

'I've never had any complaints. A few of my clients moan and scream a bit ...'

She didn't get the joke, but by now was clearly already following her own train of thought.

'Have you ever had sex on a plane?' she asked.

'No,' I said. 'But I'd like to.'

'Come on then,' she said.

She stood up quickly. By now the red signs had turned to green, and I realised that we had to catch our flight. But it was also clear that I was going to be flying a very exclusive class.

Chapter Forty-six

I followed her down the escalator and through the crowded departure lounge, admiring the sway of her walk and the shape of her legs. I couldn't see Celeste anywhere, but assumed she was old enough to find her way to a plane. We cut even the first class queue, and with a nod of the head and a wave of our documents, we were ushered on board. I dumped my stuff on a seat in first class and then followed her back down the stairs.

If you've ever worked on planes, you'll know where the crew spend the night. I hadn't, and I didn't, so was surprised to see her disappear through a little door by the stairs. Inside was a strange set of cubicles, each with a little bed in it. She locked the door behind her and nodded for me to join her.

'Isn't this, you know, unprofessional?' I asked.

'You're the one giving it for free,' she said.

We kissed, sitting on the little bed, and she unpinned her hat. I could hear passengers coming on board, and thought with glee that they wouldn't be the only ones. As she shook out her long, curly hair, I slowly unbuttoned her jacket and her blouse. We undressed each other awkwardly in the confined space, but enjoyed the closeness that the reduced dimensions imposed upon us.

Soon, she was in her underwear and I was naked. She pushed me down onto the bed and straddled me: half-naked, she looked even more French with her little lacy bra and knickers, hold-up stockings and thick high heels.

'Fuck me in Spanish, Cesc,' she said, rubbing my cock against the silk of her crotch while she rubbed her hands over my chest.

'Si insistís,' I replied, milking my accent for all it was worth.

'Ah oui,' she replied, running both hands up the sides of my penis and then bending down to suck me. I lay back and enjoyed the feeling of her thick hair falling over my body and her pout held tight against my penis. After revelling in the pleasure of her expert oral sex for a while, I sat up and guided her away from me and down, slipping off the straps of her bra as we sat up together, and then lightly kissing the smooth skin of her cleavage and breasts. Her breasts tumbled out of the bra, and I kissed and sucked her nipples while working my hand down her stomach and towards her inner thigh.

Her lacy knickers slipped aside with ease, and I gently stroked her while continuing to pleasure her breasts. I guided her down and then slid her knickers down, kissing the smooth hair of her pussy and then slipping my tongue towards her sex. She arched her back with pleasure on the first touch of my tongue against her clit, so I held back, lightly flicking over her lips and then gently putting my tongue inside her.

'You are a professional,' she whispered, before another stroke of my tongue sent her arching with pleasure once more.

As I tasted her pussy, I tried to work out a position for sex that would work in the confined space.

Eventually, just as she started the little tremors that would soon explode into the shudders of a climax, I decided that I needed to be inside her. I found a condom in my jeans, scrabbling about on the floor with my hand while keeping the other one firmly against her hips as I continued with cunnilingus. I sat back up, rolled the condom on and guided her towards my lap. The penetration was deep, tight and satisfying, and I propped the small of her back against my thighs so she could rock against my cock while I played with her breasts and gently strummed her clitoris towards her first orgasm. She came quietly but energetically, gritting her teeth and closing her eyes, and then biting hard into my shoulder at the heights of her pleasure. Then she fell back, and with my legs bent up against the end of the bed, I screwed her hard in the missionary position, her hands above her head in the little bed to stop us banging too hard.

Her second coming, harder and more violent, coincided with mine, and soon we were lying breathlessly entwined.

'I think we should get back out there for take-off,' she said.

We separated, and she adjusted her stockings and found her underwear. She was even sexier after sex, with the smell of her orgasm still in the air and her hair falling untidily about her shoulders. I dressed quickly, and she opened the door for me. As I poked my head out, I heard the captain explaining about the delay, while passengers filed on around us. I was thinking to myself that it had been a brief, although highly enjoyable fuck, when I heard the end of his announcement.

'… flight to Marseille.'

I turned to the stewardess, who was now impeccable in her uniform.

'Marseille? I'm flying to Avignon. I'm on the wrong plane.'

She let out a broad laugh at the look of panic on my face.

'Yes. You'd better run,' she said, still laughing at me.

I pushed past a couple of passengers, grabbed my bag

and charged off the plane, much to the surprise of the steward and stewardess waiting by the passenger door as the last stragglers came on board.

'Sorry,' I shouted as I went past. 'Wrong plane.'

I hadn't been far off: Celeste was at the back of the queue on the next but one gate, with a face that looked like someone had tried to feed her horse dung.

'Sorry dear,' I said breathlessly. 'I got on the wrong plane.'

Celeste looked at me, and then moved closer.

'I don't even want to know. You stink of sex.'

She refused to talk to me throughout the flight, and only began to thaw once we'd arrived in France. We made our change at Orly, while I teased her about being jealous, but she ignored me and even when we were on the second flight she continued reading in-flight magazines and bugging the crew for more drinks.

'I'm driving then, I guess,' I said to her after she sank her third vodka tonic of the short trip.

We breezed through the airport on the other side – unlike Gatwick, Avignon did not give the impression of having been struck by a meteorite – and picked up our hire car. The vehicle looked huge, a vast German 4x4, or at least it did until Celeste filled every available space with her bags, cases and duty free. I slung my stuff in the back, adjusted my shades and headed out on to the motorway.

Soon we were off the main road and winding our way along narrow, high-hedged country lanes towards V.'s villa. I'd expected something rustic and charming, but when we arrived at the gates of a modern country club I assumed that my half-drunk co-pilot had misread the map. But Celeste hadn't got us lost: V.'s villa was part of a brand-new complex, a series of luxury villas, each dotted on a secluded spot around the end of a freshly landscaped park.

We were buzzed through the gates and along a curving driveway. We passed a couple of properties, and eventually came to the entrance to V.'s place. High trees guarded the villa from prying eyes, and we climbed up a narrow approach road. After a final curve, it opened out on to a gravel car park, where I left the 4x4 between a Bentley and an expensive-looking black Citroën.

The villa was newly built but in the old style: white walls, tiled roof, looking down on to a long front lawn that ran round a crystal blue swimming pool and newly laid terrace. As I stepped out of the car, a white-suited man came out to greet us and, with the help of a smaller colleague, took our luggage.

Celeste, immediately in her element, waltzed off to get settled into her room, while I wandered round the front of the wide, low building to see if anyone was around. It was mid-morning, and the ground was scorching hot.

I found V., wearing a sarong, white bikini top and extremely wide-brimmed hat, standing by the pool, discussing cocktails with a woman I was fairly sure I recognised from television.

'Dr Aleixandre, so good of you to make it,' she said, effusively. 'Let me introduce you to a friend ...'

Chapter Forty-seven

I found Celeste in her room some time later.

V. had given us adjoining rooms towards the far corner of the villa; in reality, it was a suite with a double door, but my room had been given a bed. Despite the modernity of the construction, the style was traditional French, with concessions to the hot weather, including air conditioning to help the blinds and high windows. We had a view down into the valley on the other side of the complex, where it looked like a golf course was going to be built. A shame, I thought.

Celeste had decided to recover from the flight by trying out everything in the room, and wasted no time testing out the whirlpool bath. I thought it was a tacky feature, but judging from the delighted giggles coming from our bathroom, Celeste was in a childish heaven of her own. It was the most enthusiastic I think I'd ever seen her.

In total, there were nine or ten bedrooms, and V. had invited a handful of friends and business associates, as well as a couple of journalists. A few were there for a whole week, while some were flying in and out. I wasn't entirely sure what the deal was, but I noticed that in my room, masquerading as ornaments, were a few of her more tasteful and decorative toys. There was also a drawer under Celeste's bed with V.'s ever-so-discreet catalogue and a few of the less obviously presentable products. You don't want to scare any elderly relatives, after all.

Apart from V. and Celeste, I knew no one else there. After we'd both freshened up, and I'd made Celeste dry up some of the terrible mess she'd made on the bathroom floor, we dressed and headed back out and up on to the veranda overlooking the pool and terrace. V. was there, drinking champagne in the warm early evening, while her friend Frances, a writer, was telling her about her latest work, a book on clandestine sexual cultures in London. V. cast me a knowing look while Celeste helped herself to a drink and began telling a slightly risqué story about a former semi-boyfriend of hers who she'd discovered like to dress up as a baby. I could see Frances taking mental shorthand, and I made a note to myself to look out for this story in her future work.

As the evening arrived, so did more guests, either from their rooms or from their flights: a shy couple in their early thirties who owned an underwear emporium; a fey American designer who worked for V. and was wearing the most ridiculous safari outfit I'd ever seen; and a couple of V.'s friends, similarly well-spoken ladies in their forties who took a fascination in my work as an expert in sexual therapy. I laid on the accent as best I could, while Celeste got drunker and increasingly flirtatious with both members of the underwear-selling couple.

Two more guests, a rather pickled fifty-something novelist from Paris who'd written a best-selling book about the underworld of pimps and hookers in the French capital, and his wife, a stunning young model of Senegalese descent, arrived for dinner. I discovered that Celeste spoke French, particularly after she'd had a few drinks, and left her chatting with the model and Yuri, her writer husband, while I tried to get some idea of the form from V.

'It's simple, Cesc,' she whispered to me

conspiratorially over a glass of red wine that could have doubled as a bucket. 'I just want a few people who've been good to me to enjoy themselves. As much as possible.'

'And all the toys? Are those just for show?'

'Cesc. Don't be silly,' she replied. 'Now, do keep Frances company while I entertain Carson,' she added, leaving me to join the American designer, who was struggling to keep up conversation with the underwear people.

'So,' said Frances, 'you've really got a PhD in sex.'

'It's not quite that simple,' I said.

'And the girl? Is she your …'

'Research assistant,' I said. 'Yes.'

I studied my dinner partner. She was my age and ever so English: pale, smartly dressed, with mousy blonde hair cut into a sensible fringe. I tried to square the image I saw with an earlier book of hers that I'd read, generally involving mass orgies in seedy South London clubs.

I considered that changing the subject was a good idea if I was to keep up my disguise, and asked her about her work. She was eager to oblige, and explained to me how she'd broken into journalism, all the crap jobs she'd had, then become a writer, etc., etc. I smiled, and let my mind wander.

We were interrupted by the arrival of dessert, another sumptuous and, I noticed, extremely sticky dish. We'd had early oysters, and asparagus with our beef, and now something chocolatey that would be best spread and licked off, all served with highly drinkable but very alcoholic wines.

'Do you notice,' I said to Frances, 'that we're being fed up for sex?'

'You really are the professional,' she replied.

239

I nodded. She didn't know quite how right she was.

Nothing out of the ordinary happened that night: Celeste was positively legless by the time we retired to the lounge, so I helped her to bed as she made giggling, drunken apologies to all. At about two in the morning, the sound of energetic fucking filtered through the door of my room. Having ascertained that it wasn't Celeste frotting herself, I pulled on some shorts and went out to investigate, wondering if there might be some fun to be had. Along the corridor I identified the guilty room: grunts and squeals in French were emerging from behind the double door, and I soon identified the culprits as the novelist and his beautiful companion. I tried to banish the image from my head, and headed back to my room.

The next morning, similar noises could be heard coming from the room belonging to the young underwear millionaires, who'd clearly decided to start the second day of their holiday with a bang. They'd seemed nice enough during our brief exchanges: Jake and Jenny. He'd been in finance, and she'd worked in sales, until they'd decided to set up a little boutique in West London selling high-end lingerie. The business had taken off, and they proudly and only half-jokingly referred to themselves as knicker-millionaires.

The day passed idly by: I sunbathed while Celeste hid her hangover behind her shades before spending the afternoon prancing around in a string bikini so tiny it would have been expelled from Brazil. I noticed the Parisian novelist taking a shine to her, while I chatted to his young wife, who looked stunning in a miniscule emerald green all-in-one outfit. I challenged her to a swimming race, but she refused with a broad smile, so I dived into the clear waters and paddled fairly aimlessly before joining the others for lunch indoors.

After lunch I got talking to V.'s friends back out on the terrace, both of whom I fancied as possible clients, and then by the afternoon we started another round of cocktails in the sun. V. and her designer spent much of the day talking business with a sketch pad and a few examples of her wares on a glass table in the shade of a corner close to the house. As the heat rose, I made my excuses and headed inside for a siesta.

In the cool of the house, I bumped into Frances. She'd set up in one of the little alcoves off the big dining room and was tapping away at her laptop.

'Working holiday, eh?' I asked, surprising her.

She started and gave a turn.

'Sorry, 'fraid so, got a deadline to make.'

'What are you writing about?'

'Differences between the French and the British.'

I caught sight of the novelist and the model ducking between the pillars towards their room, while Jake and Jenny emerged from what looked like an energetic afternoon siesta.

'I don't think they're that great, you know,' I said, with a smile.

'Perhaps. But that doesn't make for a great chapter. Listen, later, I'd like to ask you about your work. Would you be interested in giving an interview? I can pay.'

'I don't think so. My work is much more academic,' I answered, giving her a bow of the head as I headed off to the room.

I slept soundly in the chill of my room, with the hum of the air conditioning lulling me to sleep. Hours must have passed, as my next memory was of being hit with a pillow.

'Cesc, wake up you lazy sod. Dinner's in half an hour.'

241

It was Celeste, tipsy, flirtatious and looking rather sexy in her bikini and sun hat.

'I'll get dressed,' I said, as she headed off to her room to chuck clothes around.

V. had warned me that the Friday dinner would be a more formal affair, so after a shower I slung on a shirt and a jacket. As I joined the others, I noticed that formal meant all things to all people: the novelist had trimmed his beard into an elegant shape and was sporting what can only be called a smoking jacket. His wife wore a floor-length gown. V.'s friends had chosen cocktail dresses, and Frances was in a little black dress. Celeste eventually emerged straight from the 1980s in a puffball skirt with her hair backcombed six inches above her head. I was impressed. Last to emerge were the underwear millionaires, he in a casual suit, she a floaty summer dress that suited her otherwise nondescript, boyish shape.

Over dinner, two lines of conversation kept returning: Jake insisted that he'd met Celeste, or recognised her from somewhere, and Frances talked about her writing, and how much she'd like to incorporate this into her book somehow. The novelist joked that he had already stolen it for his next work.

'What is it that you find so interesting about the situation?' asked V.

He looked at her. 'The dispositive is so flexible. We could have a murder. We could have an orgy. Or we could have a great confession.'

Meanwhile, at the other end of the table, Jake and Jenny were running through with Celeste all the possible degrees of separation: whether she'd made a purchase with them, or done modelling for them, whether she had any model friends. I could see Celeste getting more and more tipsy and exasperated, and I thought about rescuing her. Meanwhile, I tried to flirt with the Senegalese model – Dieudonnée was her marvellous name – but she was well practised in fending off such attractions, and besides, I was sitting between her and Frances, who was keenly trying to find out as much about my work as possible.

I put off giving anything away as best as I could. But it was a tricky task, made more so by the combination of the heavy wine, the heady scent of perfume in the air, and V.'s clever hosting. After dinner, seductive music began to play from an invisible source, and she led us upstairs and encouraged us to dance, leading Yuri the novelist to the floor for some slightly comedic turns. I found myself swaying on the veranda with Frances, who was a subtle but skilled mover. I felt her hands toying with the hair at my nape, and her breath against my neck, and I struggled to stop an erection. Meanwhile, Celeste had replaced V. and was being half-climbed up by Yuri, while continuing a strange conversation with Jake and Jenny.

It took a break in the music for the penny to drop. We had sat back on the armchairs along the veranda. Frances was on my knee, only half jokingly, while Yuri, Celeste and the couple formed a tight group next to us. Dieudonnée and the designer were in a corner, talking about art, while V. and her friends flitted between groups. Suddenly, Jake slapped a palm to his forehead.

'It's your voice!' he said to Celeste. 'I recognise your voice.'

I saw Celeste's look of surprise.

She looked at me.

Jake continued. 'You do voice-overs, right?'

'Not quite,' said Celeste, with a sheepish grin.

Suddenly, a series of pieces fell into place: the sex noises coming from Celeste's room when she was on her own. The lengthy spells holed up in her room with the phone. The phone bill that we'd actually made a profit on, and that Celeste had taken away from me as soon as I'd opened it. Her mystery source of private income.

I looked at her. I knew I shouldn't break her secret. But I couldn't resist.

'And you have a go at me!' I said.

'What?' she replied, accusingly. Around us, our fellow guests were looking bewildered.

'Cesc, she's not the only one with a secret,' said V., smiling cheekily.

'I have a confession,' said Celeste, pushing her shades further up into her hair.

'Oh I love confessions,' announced Jenny. Jake turned to me with a broad smile, while I could see Frances trying to memorise the details.

'I'm not a researcher. In fact, neither is he,' she added.

'Thanks, Celeste, I'm glad you can keep a secret.'

'The reason why you recognise my voice is that you've probably rung me.'

Jenny gave Jake a quizzical look, while realisation crossed his face.

'Shit,' he said. 'I knew I'd heard that name before.'

'I do sex chat.'

Yuri looked slightly confused. 'Sex chat?' he said.

'Phone lines,' I clarified. 'Celeste does rude phone lines.'

I was amazed to discover that Celeste had such an interesting little sideline. I'd always suspected that her mysterious income was either a trust fund, or her doing the same thing I do with a certain sort of wealthy, older gentleman. In fact, it was something rather more mundane, but on the other hand, just spicy enough for her to be embarrassed at us all finding out.

For a while I'd just thought that she was masturbating a lot.

'Celeste, I don't understand. You just sound bored. Is that how you market yourself: slightly uninterested sex chat?'

'Cesc, you're not funny. Now, everyone, do you want to know the other secret here?' Celeste continued. Jake clapped his hands while Frances beamed at me.

'OK, OK,' I interrupted. 'It's very simple. I'm not, well, I'm not exactly who V. has told you I am.' I half expected to be interrupted by an irate hostess, but she and her friends were standing up, hanging on every word of the exchange.

'I'm not an academic. And I don't specialise in sex therapy. Well, not exactly.'

'So what do you do, then?' asked one of V.'s friends.

'I'm a call guy.' The expression was met with general incomprehension. 'I fuck women for money.'

'Brilliant,' shouted Frances, patting me on the back. 'Did you know this all?' she said, turning to face our hostess.

'Of course. Why do you think he's here? I'm only disappointed he hasn't got on with any work yet,' said V., with an ever-so-slightly superior tone in her voice.

The music struck up, while someone announced that there was cause for celebration. I even heard champagne corks popping, and in the confusion, slipped away with Celeste and led her to the balcony.

'Are you alright?' I asked.

'Yes, of course,' she said, with a laugh.

'I don't know why you didn't tell me. We're sort of in

the same profession,' I said. She cast me a mocking look.

'Only sort of, Cesc, only sort of.'

'Does it pay well?' I asked.

'Oh yes. Very well. You'd be amazed.'

I nodded and looked around me. 'Do you think our hostess is trying to arrange an orgy here?' I asked.

'Oh yes,' replied Celeste. 'And I think your job is to start it.'

'I think you're probably right,' I said. I left her and returned to the others. I held out a hand to Frances the journalist, and we danced for a while.

V. came over and joined us.

'Apparently, it's my job to start an orgy,' I whispered to her.

'You could do worse,' she said. With Frances's hand still in mine, I moved closer to V.

'Just one question,' I said.

'What?' she answered.

'Why all the subterfuge? Are you hiding something?'

'Oh no. Subterfuge just makes it more interesting.'

'Is this legal?'

'Which aspect?'

'Erm, all of it.'

'Well, probably not the tax bit.'

'What do you mean?'

'Well, technically, this is a works do.'

I smiled as she continued.

'I'm not sure about the rest. Why not just try?'

V. slid away with a smile, leaving me with Frances. I spun her towards me with the music.

'Apparently, it's my job to start an orgy,' I whispered to her, close to her ear, holding her close to me.

'Start one with me, if you like,' she whispered back,

biting my earlobe as she did. She sashayed off, away from me and towards the stairs down to the bedrooms. I caught up with her and caught her hand. The underwear couple got the message, and followed behind us, while I saw Celeste turning her attentions to one of the staff.

Let's just say that I did my job.

Chapter Forty-eight

Some time in the small hours of the next morning, I crawled back into my own bedroom. Frances followed me, leaving the wreckage of her own room, where champagne bottles, clothes, half-naked bodies and a few abandoned sex toys were littered over every surface. We curled up together in my bed and slept.

Despite the hangover and the lack of sleep, I woke with the sun, and wandered out into the gardens, enjoying the chill of the sprinklers in the air and the cool of the grass on my feet. Back in the room, I showered, making sure to wake up Celeste, who swore at me through the door. I was surprised to see the door open and Yuri scuttle through it. I couldn't remember at quite which stage that particular coupling had begun.

Frances was curled catlike in the bed, so I went back out to the kitchen and had one of the staff bring some coffee and juice.

As she woke, bleary eyed, it was clear that her writer's brain had been working overdrive.

'You'll have to change the names,' I said, before she'd even begun to speak.

'Not everything's a story,' she said.

'But this is, isn't it?'

She shrugged, the sheets falling to reveal the smooth curves of her breasts. It was hard to reconcile the demure image she cast that first morning with the woman I'd seen going down on Dieudonnée while I'd screwed her from behind.

'I suspect my editor might want to cut some of the more scandalous bits.'

She sipped her coffee and then looked at me.

'Why the lie?' she asked.

'It was V.'s idea.'

'Are you embarrassed?'

'I'm more embarrassed about the lie than getting found out. I'm not ashamed of my job, that's for sure. I guess I just don't go round shouting about it. It's not quite as respectable as some careers.'

'You must have some great stories,' she said, searching around on the floor for some cigarettes.

'I guess so. But it's strictly confidential. My clients mostly pay me for discretion.'

She gave me a long look as she finally lit her cigarette.

'Whatever you do, make sure I give you a card, OK?'

'Why? Do you want to put some work my way?' I said.

She nodded. 'Perhaps. Perhaps.'

The next few days were less dramatic: Frances decided that she preferred my bed to anyone else's, and we spent long afternoons and nights making love, interrupted only occasionally by shouts from Celeste telling us to keep the noise down. The other couples settled back into something rather more normal, with frequent noisy orgasms emerging from Yuri and Dieudonnée, who seemed to have decided to make up for their night apart with ever more frantic screwing. I have a strong suspicion that Celeste may have snuck out of her room one night to screw one of the kitchen staff, but I can't be sure. After a couple more days, everyone in the group seemed to act like old friends, so it was a surprise when we started going our separate ways.

I took Frances's card, but back in the UK didn't get round to calling her. It felt for all the world like a holiday romance, and I had no interest in being the main subject of a chapter in a book about Perverted London, or whatever she was going to call it. I also didn't think that I could really try to charge her, having already given her a whole series of freebies. I looked her up on the Internet a few times, but found no mention of those few days in France.

Over the next few weeks I found myself with some more time on my hands. Work settled down into something like a regular pattern, and I'll confess that the number of new assignments started to slow down. It might be, you never know, something to do with the credit crunch, although when Celeste suggested this to me, I pointed out that I didn't give credit.

In the meantime, I thought about Frances, and about Yuri, and realised that it would be worth jotting down a few things here and there, just in case I ever decided to write my memoirs.

One day, as I arrived at the flat, back from an assignment, I found Celeste reading something on screen. She looked up, shocked, slightly red faced.

'What's wrong with you?' she asked.

'Nothing. I've had a shocker. I ended up doing a Banksy out of the window when the Jen's husband came home.'

'Right,' she said, hastily closing what I realised was my laptop.

'Celeste, what are you doing?' I asked.

'I never realised you kept a diary.'

'You shouldn't read that,' I said, clicking the lid shut and taking the machine away from her. But as I did, I noticed something curious. She had on a dressing gown and little else. I'd clearly caught her up to something.

'Celeste, what were you doing?'

'Nothing. You know,' she said, 'some of this is pretty funny.'

'Funny?' I asked. 'Were you reading it for comedy?'

'Sort of,' she said, pulling her robe around her.

'Sort of? Admit it. It turns you on.'

Celeste looked embarrassed, and then stuck on her most brazen face.

'Well, if you ask,' she said. 'I must confess that I did consider, well, using some images as inspiration.'

Celeste had been masturbating to my diary. I was appalled. But also really rather touched.

'You were thinking about me, Celeste? How sweet.'

The End

252